Ghost Hunter

Cleveland Ohio Ghos.

Haunted Cleveland, Cuyahoga County and Vicinity

By Jannette Quackenbush

Check out other Ohio Ghost Hunter Guides:

Haunted Hocking—A Ghost Hunter's Guide to the Hocking Hills I
(Covers the Hocking Hills Region)

Haunted Hocking— A Ghost Hunter's Guide II
(Hocking Hills and the counties of Athens, Lawrence, Meigs, Fairfield, Perry, Ross, Vinton, and Scioto)

Ohio Ghost Hunter's Guide — Haunted Hocking III
(Covers Counties of: Allen, Athens, Delaware, Franklin, Gallia, Hancock, Henry, Highland, Hocking, Jackson, Lake, Licking, Lorain, Lucas, Marion, Muskingum, Perry, Pike, Sandusky, Scioto, Washington and Wood)

Ohio Ghost Hunter Guide—Franklin County IV
(Covers Columbus and Vicinity)

Ohio Ghost Hunter Guide —Haunted Hocking V
(Covers Allen, Auglaize, Butler, Champaign, Clark, Clinton, Crawford, Cuyahoga, Delaware, Franklin, Gallia, Greene, Hardin, Highland, Hocking, Jackson, Jefferson, Knox, Lake, Lawrence, Logan, Lucas, Madison, Miami, Mahoning, Montgomery, Morgan, Muskingum, Pickaway, Pike, Putnam, Richland, Ross, Sandusky, Scioto, Stark, Summit, Vinton, Warren, and Wood)

Ohio Ghost Hunter Guide —Haunted Hocking VI
(Covers Adams, Ashtabula, Belmont, Brown, Clark, Clermont, Coshocton, Cuyahoga, Defiance, Delaware, Erie, Fairfield, Fayette, Fulton, Greene, Guernsey, Hamilton, Hancock, Henry, Hocking, Jackson, Knox, Marion, Medina, Morrow, Pickaway, Pike, Sandusky, Scioto, Summit, Tuscarawas, Vinton, Warren, Wayne)

Cleveland Ohio Ghost Hunter Guide —Haunted Hocking VII
(Haunted Cleveland, Cuyahoga County and Vicinity)

ISBN-10: 1940087104
ISBN-13: 978-1-940087-10-8

21 Crows Dusk to Dawn Publishing, 21 Crows, LLC

Cover Image of Cleveland: Alex Grichenko

Disclaimer: The stories and legends in this book are for enjoyment purposes and taken from many different resources. Many have been passed down and have been altered along the way. The authors attempt to sort through the many different variations found on a story and find the most popular and the most supported by historical evidence. Not all sources and legends can be substantiated. We try to give you the basic research and history so you can delve into the stories, enjoy them, discover something new.

Potential Ghost Hunters should always respect the areas to search out the paranormal and also respect those who are still living who might be related to the dead. Public properties may become private after the printing of the book or they may simply be listed with the address so you know where the story originated. Listing the GPS and address does not imply you are welcome to visit, nor that you visit without contacting the property owner. It is to give you a visual of the location where the haunting occurred. Call ahead of time to make sure you are not trespassing. By setting the example and seeking permission and leaving areas better than what we found, we can pave the way for more ghost hunting experiences for all.

Ghost hunting can be a dangerous endeavor due to the many different environmental factors including many that are done in the darkness, forests, in old buildings or in hazardous areas. Before visiting any haunted site, verify location, accessibility and safety. We never recommend venturing into unknown areas in darkness or entering private or public property without prior permission. GPS routes may change or become hazardous. Always check with owners/operators of public and private areas to see if a license is needed to hunt and to check for unsafe areas. Make sure you follow all laws and abide by the rules of any private or public region you use. Readers assume full responsibility for use of information in this book.

The background images were taken at the actual site of the haunted area, if applicable and available. Other images were added to illustrate what others have seen. Oh, and none of the ghosts or ghost hunters were hurt while making this book. Some of the images just look like it. For those who would like to share their ghost story occurring in Ohio or surrounding states, contact us through hauntedhocking.com. We would love to hear from you!

Table of Contents—Ghost Hunter Guide

Table of Contents—Ghost Hunter Guide

Table of Contents—Ghost Hunter Guide

Cleveland Ohio Ghost Hunter Guide
Haunted Cleveland, Cuyahoga County and Vicinity

Calvary Cemetery
10000 Miles Avenue
Cleveland, Ohio 44105
41.441393,-81.602836

Cuyahoga County

Shadows of a 1918 Epidemic

Calvary Cemetery is the largest Catholic Cemetery in Cleveland and was dedicated in 1893.

With over 305,000 burials it has to be expected at least a few who have been laid to rest here have decided to come back and walk the hallowed land above their graves. The largest number of burials in a single day was on November 4, 1918 when 81 people were buried within because of the influenza epidemic. In fact, after the epidemic where over 4,400 citizens of Cleveland died, people began noticing shadow figures lurking about the graves and tiny lights bobbing around.

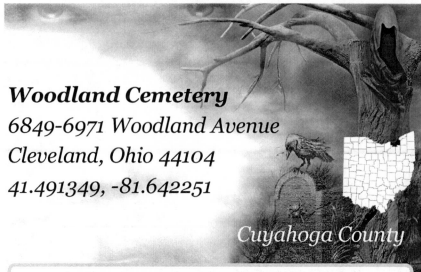

Woodland Cemetery

6849-6971 Woodland Avenue
Cleveland, Ohio 44104
41.491349, -81.642251

Cuyahoga County

> **Sometimes the Not-So-Scary is Far More Terrifying Than the Truly Scary**

Ghost hunters come in every shape, size, age, personality. . . and fear threshold. The passion to discover evidence of ghostly phenomenon, to take the adventure into a dark cemetery doesn't deny anyone access based on their appearance, personality or even reaction when coming face to face with a real ghost.

Still, although anyone can grab up a flashlight and take a step toward the wrought iron gates and nearly to the lines of old, broken headstones within, not all will have the courage to pass through them. There will always be those faint of heart who will simply peer within. Others will turn and walk away.

But those who will remain, who cross the bounds into the graveyards to seek out their adventure, they are the brave who will find the truth someday. Their names will welcome the accolade at their feat. Or . . . maybe not.

The Ghost Discovered!—*Last evening a party of resolute fellow, armed with clubs, bowie-knives and revolvers, started out on a search for the ghost. They patrolled the streets in the vicinity of the cemetery for several hours. About midnight one of the party who had got a little ahead of his fellows, ran back, hatless and pale with fright, exclaiming, "I have seen him! I have seen the Ghost!" His comrades were seized with a sudden trembling and showed a disposition to run. One suddenly remembered an engagement that he had downtown and started on a run to fulfill it. Another said that he had been up late for several nights and he "thought he'd go home," and away he scampered also. The remainder held a consultation and concluded to investigate at all hazards. They cocked their revolvers, loosened their knives, and grasping their clubs more firmly, crept stealthily, with chattering teeth, to the spot indicated. They peered through cracks in the fence inclosing the yard, and the horrible spectre was revealed to them, swinging its weird arms in the moonlight, and nodding its bead in a most diabolical manner. All immediately took to their heels except one bold fellow who determined to ascertain whether his Ghostship was flesh and blood or not. He sprang over the fence, club in hand. The spectre did not retreat but continued to swing its arms and nod its head mockingly. Choking down his fear the man raised his club resolutely and aimed a crushing blow fairly at the spectre's head. Down went the ghost and down went the ghost hunter, for his club met with but little resistance. Horror stricken he regained his feet, when lo! he found that the Ghost was a woman's night gown which had been left out on a clothes line. A night-cap pinned on the line at the top of the garment was what appeared to the excited imagination of the ghost hunters to be the spectre's head. None of that party desire to have the papers say anything about it and they probably wont.* **Cleveland morning Leader.**

Cleveland, Ohio.

December 05, 1862.

The Ghost Discovered!

Woodland Cemetery
6849-6971 Woodland Avenue
Cleveland, Ohio 44104
41.491349, -81.642251

Cuyahoga County

An Unhappy Ghost —
Joseph Tompkins

Lot 83, Tier 5, Grave 44.

There is   lonely section of graveyard in Woodland Cemetery where many of the wooden markers once revealing the names of the dead beneath are long rotted away like the flesh and bones of those each identified. The engraved names on the old marble and granite headstones have been rubbed away by spring rains and snowy winters. Families and friends and old acquaintances once visiting the graves are long dead themselves. Only the sound of birds, loud car mufflers and those still living in the apartments nearby waver close enough to call any attention to those within this old section of cemetery. Vague, coffin-shaped indentations in the dirt are the only proof left divulging the truth someone was once buried there at all.

Most likely, no one even knows Joseph Tomkins (also spelled, Thomkins and Thompkins) is one of those buried beneath the indented bit of soil and grass among a handful of others just like it on Lot 83, Tier 5 and grave number 44. They seem to go on forever. Well, that is, except those who might be delving into old newspapers to discover a tiny treasure of a story buried in the historical archives of the February 2, 1913 Cleveland Plain Dealer. And it is about an unhappy, lost ghost that haunted a woman, whether she wanted to be haunted or not . . .

. . . On Feb. 14, 1854, according to the records of Woodland cemetery, a large lot was purchased there by James Lawrence. No one was interred immediately following the purchase of the lot nor in fact during the first year that it stood in the Lawrence name. But on the 15th day of February, 1855, in a grave prepared under authority from James Lawrence, Joseph Thompkins was buried there, thus becoming the first occupant of the Lawrence lot.

Whether he was a relative, a friend of the family or a mere acquaintance, or whether he was only a stranger given burial space through the kindness of heart of James Lawrence, the lot's rightful owner, the records do not state. Thompkins was a young man, aged 39, as the records say, and he died of consumption.

No grave markers were ever placed, and as the years passed the mound of earth that marked his resting place smoothed itself to the level of the earth about it, and the grave was lost sight of. Only in the records of the cemetery was there anything to show that Joseph Thompkins had ever lived. No one came to make inquiry concerning him or to look for his grave.

*Twenty years passed, with Thompkins the only occupant of the lot, when it changed ownership, the Lawrence family selling it to Jacob Hoffman. No mention of the lonely grave was made to Jacob Hoffman when he bought the lot; he purchased it believing it was unused. When the soil was turned to make place for a second tenant, Thompkins was only slightly disturbed. True, it worried his spirit somewhat to see that his own grave had completely vanished from view; but that was as nothing to the perturbation that became his later as by degrees vacant spaces were opened and other silent tenants slipped into places allotted to them, each new grave leaving less ground to be chosen from for those that would follow, each one coming nearer and nearer still to where Thompkins lay, forgotten, with nothing to show that a grave had been . . . **Cleveland Plain Dealer. February 2, 1913. Who'll Make This Ghost Happy—Historical Archives.***

But in November of 1912, a Swiss immigrant by the name of Mary Pauli who now lived in Cleveland was in for a great surprise. During a séance , a tall, distinguished young man with long dark hair and a military-type coat appeared to a medium in spirit form. He told Mary Pauli through the medium that his name was Joseph Tomkins. He also told her about his unmarked grave in Woodland Cemetery and his fear that his bones, being moved around once in a while, would be accidently tossed in the dump and lost forever. Joseph Tomkins begged of her to find the obscure place his body lay and to make sure it was properly marked.

The Hoffman Lot where Joseph Tomkins was originally buried on February 15, 1855. Mary Pauli had a marker put in place at section: 8, Lot: 44, Grave: 1. On October 14, 1914, records show the body was boxed and moved to Section: 67, Tier: 7, Grave:27. A 3rd reburial appeared to be made on December 26, 1914 to Lot 83 Tier: 5 Grave: 44.

And so she did. Mary Pauli made her way to Woodland Cemetery and told the cemetery workers about the mislaid grave. And after a bit of digging into the old archives, they found the actual record of Mister Tomkins being buried in a far corner of the Hoffman lot. She paid the Woodland Cemetery officials to place a marker there for the burial plot, then went away content her promise had been kept to Mister Tomkins.

The ghost seemed happy too. And all was good until the Hoffmans found a stranger suddenly buried in their lot. They demanded the man's bones be dug up and placed in another part of the cemetery. And so, the cemetery grave diggers got out their shovels and began to excavate.

They dug up old pieces of a casket right where Mary Pauli had asked them to place the marker, along with the bones of a very tall man with long dark hair and a military-type coat. On December 26th, they placed Joseph Tomkins's bones into a small box and reburied him in a different part of the cemetery, where single allotment graves were placed.

> . . . On Friday, Jan 3, Mrs. Pauli visited the medium and Thompkins' spirit at once appeared and told his tale of woe. "I am miserable, much worse off than ever before. I am actually uncomfortable, they have dug me up out of my roomy grave, and have put me in a little bit of a box; my legs are twisted out of shape, they are tossed in upside down; I cannot rest; do something to help me," the wraith implored her.
>
> On Saturday, Jan. 4, Mrs. Pauli again went to Woodland cemetery, and asked why she had not been summoned when Thompkins' own rightful grave was opened up, so that she could see for herself the handling and transfer of all that was mortal of her spirit friend. How and where had they laid him, she asked.
>
> "Every bone carefully picked up and packed neatly in a little three-foot box, transferred to grave 27, section 67, tier 7 in the single grave allotment," cemetery officials read from the new records and told her.
>
> "But the man is not satisfied; that grave was his grave; he had rested there fifty-eight years, he should not have been removed, or if removed he should have been placed together straight and clean in a new casket, and given room in as good a part of the cemetery as that from which he was taken," Mrs. Pauli insists. For poor Thompkins is really wretched now! Ghosts are not snobbish, but Thompkins was an occupant of the aristocratic side of Woodland cemetery; now he rests side by side with nameless, unmarked graves. His is the only one of seven almost touching that bears a marker, and that only a pine board with the name Joseph Thompkins painted on. Thompkins' pride is hurt. He is indeed an unhappy wraith. But what can be done? . . .
>
> **Cleveland Plain Dealer. February 2, 1913. Who'll Make This Ghost Happy—Historical Archives.**

However, Missus Pauli was told if the man was to be reburied, she would have to pay for the burial, the casket and putting the bones back together herself.

. . . If Mrs. Pauli wishes to buy another lot and buy a new casket to hold his bones, he can be removed again at her expense. No one except a person well versed in anatomy could fit together correctly one by one those old half-crumbling bones. They could be put together, wired and Thompkins made into a presentable skeleton, cemetery attendants say; but it would be a tedious and costly job. "I am desperate and helpless now, I do not know what further I can do; it seems to me poor Thompkins will simply have to content himself," Mrs. Pauli says.

Who was Joseph Thompkins? At present his status is clear; he is merely an unhappy ghost. But in real life fifty-eight years ago? "He was a physician, and of high standing, I am certain, he has told me so," declares Mrs. Pauli. Thompkins death occurred on York-st, cemetery records say. Old Cleveland directories of that date do not show that either a Lawrence or Thompkins family resided on York-st. Mrs. Pauli's acquaintance with Thompkins dates no further back than the spirit meeting of November, 1912. She is 62 now, so when Thompkins died at the age of 39, fifty-eight years ago, she was a baby of 4. . . **Cleveland Plain Dealer. February 2, 1913. Who'll Make This Ghost Happy—Historical Archives.**

      Mrs. Pauli stood by her word the unhappy spirit of Joseph Tomkins was real. It would be hard to dispute her concise description of his body and clothing, the exact place where he was buried. His genuine records can be found at Woodland Cemetery, along with the reburial from the upper class family plot at Lot 8 to the single burial plots at Lot 83. His grave is still unmarked, his body still decaying in the tiny box he was placed in December 26th of 1912. And his ghost? He will probably never rest well until someone puts his bones back together, in a tall casket back in the Hoffman lot where he believes they belong.

Old Farmer's Market Alley

1979 W 25th Street
Cleveland, Ohio 44113
41.484821,-81.703653

Cuyahoga County

Black Mary Ann

New West Side Market House, Cleveland, Ohio.

The market has been in this section of town since 1840 so there has been plenty of time to work up at least one spirit to add to Cleveland's haunted history.

A woman murdered in the 1930s walks the alleyways near the West Side Market, searching for her killer. She wears a black cape and creeps through the darkness, blending into the buildings and brick roadways.

Cleveland, Ohio
Kingsbury Run and Vicinity

Cuyahoga County

Mad Butcher of Kingsbury Run

Kingsbury Run, 1930s.

Kingsbury Run, early 1900s.

Photos Courtesy: Cleveland State University, Cleveland Memory Project

The ghosts of thirteen victims and the ghost of a serial killer roam the desolate crooks and crannies of Cleveland. They've been witnessed on a rugged shoreline beach. They have been seen along a grassy incline called Jackass Hill strewn with buckled chain link fence and matted with old car tires and assorted trash. They are the remnants of a bygone time in the mid-1930s. It was a time and a place when the down-and-out made their way to a section of the city called Kingsbury Run, a shanty town along the winding creek bed that ran to the Cuyahoga River.

It was between 1934 and 1938, the city of Cleveland was terrorized by an unknown serial killer known as The Mad Butcher of Kingsbury Run. During his four year reign of terror, the Mad Butcher was believed to have murdered at least 13 people. As with most serial killers, other than being recognized as having psychopathic tendencies, he had a trademark leading local police to tie his victims together—The Mad Butcher of Kingsbury Run decapitated his victims, most while still alive. Many of the bodies were also dismembered, leaving only the torso in one area and the remaining body parts in another area. Some were found in burlap sacks and wrapped in either brown cardboard or local newspapers. Others were simply found dumped along the Lake Erie shoreline and the Cuyahoga River.

Rivaling the murdering, mutilating spree of Jack the Ripper, this faceless, nameless person killed and dismembered thirteen males and females who either lived among or mingled with those in a shanty-town district of Cleveland—drifters, prostitutes, hobos and even families left homeless during the depression. The murders were never solved. There was never enough evidence against any one suspect to make a solid case. Most of the bodies were found in Kingsbury Run—a slum in the eastern section of Cleveland that made a jagged lope where old stone quarries and an ancient creek bed once existed with beautiful ravines.

Euclid Beach, then and now. Two bodies were found washed up here— In 1934, the Lady of the Lake.

In 1937, Jane Doe V was found here on the beach near 156th Street and East 30th Street.

GPS: 41.583077,-81.570615

GPS: 41.58258,-81.570894

But by the 1930s near the rutted Erie and Nickel Plate railroad tracks, the land had become a desolate area of dumps and wasteland and an easy place for squatters and the homeless to set up camps. It was also an easy place for a serial killer to find his prey and an easy place for this human butcher to dump his victim's remains. The expanse of his hunting ground was large. Kingsbury Run ran the eastern section of Shaker Heights and west through Kinsman Avenue and all the way to the Cuyahoga River.

When the first victim washed up on the shoreline of Euclid Beach on September 5, 1934, no one anticipated the corpse would be one in a long line of murdered and mutilated males and females found strewn about isolated areas of Cleveland over the next four years. Twenty-one year-old Frank La Gossie had been taking a stroll along the shore. He was picking up driftwood when he saw something odd sticking out of the sand along the beach. Upon closer inspection and to his horror, the strange object was a human torso. Later given the name 'Lady of the Lake', and not actually included in some counts as a victim of the Butcher of Kingsbury, the method used to kill this victim and the mutilation would be nearly identical to the other victims found over the next four years. The body found by La Gossie had both arms and head missing. Her legs were cut off at the knees.

On February 23, 1937 a second headless woman would be found in the same area as Lady of the Lake. But it was only over a year and a month from Lady of the Lake's discovery, when on September 23, 1935, two boys were playing in a remote area near the tracks of Kingsbury Run, a graceful rift in the hillside often used by area children for sledding. One of the boys ran down the hillside, racing the other to the grassy bottom. Neither expected to stop in shock after eyeing a parcel of clothing sticking out of the brush. One poke of a stick and they recognized it as a man. Or what was left of him. His head and male organs were missing. Nearby, another male body was found with identical mutilations. Only his socks were left on his feet. The first body was never identified. His age was only estimated as between 35 and 40.

GPS: 41.478888,-81.656845 (Andrassy)
GPS:41.478882,-81.656847 (John Doe I)

Jackass Hill: Near the end of Praha Avenue. Edward Andrassy, pictured above, was one of the victims found on the hill in 1935.

The second body, however, would be what police would label as the first identified murder victim of the Butcher. His name was Edward W. Andrassy– age 28 divorced, out of work and one time worked at a psychiatric ward. He had been arrested for public intoxication in the past along with carrying a concealed weapon. He was not well liked, and from hearsay, more than a few people had threatened to kill him. Andrassy had done time at Warrensville Workhouse.

1937   Lorain-Carnegie Bridge (Hope Memorial Bridge). Jane Doe VI, was the only African American victim recovered. She was found wrapped in a burlap sack in a newspaper by teenagers watching boats.

41.49331, -81.687988

1938 Lakeshore Dumps - 9th Street Downtown Jane Doe IX and John Doe X found in the water.

41.510377, -81.693707

Photo right Courtesy: Cleveland State University, Cleveland Memory Project

As the next four years passed, the Mad Butcher of Kingsbury Run would leave his terrible mark with seven male and five female victims. The last would be two victims fished out of the Lakeshore Dump in downtown Cleveland in August of 1938. Then just as suddenly as the murders began, they seemed to end. No one was ever convicted of the murders. Psychiatric analysis described the murderer as someone with slaughtering skills like a butcher or someone with medical skills such as a doctor, veterinarian or medical

1936—Area of Kingsbury Run: Where the Tattoo Man was found.

41.480354,-81.643059

student—someone, the county coroner described, who had enough skill to dissect with finesse. The Butcher was believed to be large enough to carry his victims, and right handed. Police believed he gained the trust of his victims before they were murdered. They also believed most of the victims were poor and unknown with no families who would miss them.

Examining

evidence of the murders.

Photo Courtesy: Cleveland State University, Cleveland Memory Project

There were many suspects which included:

- *Dr. Frank E. Sweeney*, a veteran of a World War I unit who conducted amputations in the field. He quickly admitted himself into the Sandusky Veteran's Hospital in 1938 when the bodies began to be discovered.

-*Frank Dolezal* (center), a 32 year-old bricklayer, allegedly admitted to one murder, then recanted saying he had been beaten by local police until he confessed.

Courtesy: Cleveland State University,

Although the railroad tracks still remain, the shanty houses of Kingsbury Run are gone. Only weedy patches, buckled streets filled with old factories, buildings and houses running along the highway are a reminder of the old shanty town of Kingsbury Run. But they say the ghost of the Mad Butcher of

Kingsbury Run still roams the area searching for his victims old and new. And so do his victims where their bodies were dumped.

And perhaps he is. On July 22, 1950 the body of 41 year-old Robert Robertson was found to fit the same profile as those murdered

A section of Kingsbury now.

Death mask of Robert Robertson. Courtesy: Cleveland State University, Cleveland Memory Project

nearly 15 years earlier. Some believe it was not just an isolated case and perhaps, is connected with the murders. Scary, huh?

Squire's Castle
2300 River Road
Willoughby, Ohio 44094
41.581175,-81.418703

Cuyahoga County

Squire's Castle

Squire's Castle was built in the late 1890s by Feargus Squire, an oil magnate and associate of John D. Rockefeller. Feargus had amassed a pretty good fortune and wanted a country house within arms-reach of Willoughby, but still out in the wilderness. He started by erecting a gatekeeper house. He then hired a landscaper and had paths, roads and trails added to the 525 acres so work could begin on the larger estate.

There was only one thing coming between him and his outdoor refuge. And that would be his wife, Rebecca Squire. She refused to live there, far from her friends and family and without the typical fare of the city. So work was stopped and the building simply used as a weekend getaway for the family. The house eventually lay empty and was donated to Cleveland Metroparks.

For many years, there was a legend surrounding the building that Squire's wife, Rebecca, fell near the fireplace and died tragically. Her ghost could be seen staring from the windows. Although she did not die there, strangely, rumors still persist that a ghost lingers at the gatekeeper house.

The Drury Mansion
8625 Euclid Avenue
Cleveland, Ohio 44106
41.503592,-81.62651

Cuyahoga County

Flaming Woman of Drury Mansion

Francis Drury Mansion, 1912. Photo Courtesy: Cleveland State University, Cleveland Memory Project

A mansion on Millionaire's Row in Cleveland, a paroled prisoner and a horrendous fire at a hospital. No one would have thought all three would collide together one night in the 1970s. They had nothing truly in common except for perhaps two things. One was the street they all occurred on and the other, it was a ghost.

At a few seconds after 11:30 a.m. on May 15, 1929, catastrophe would strike the Cleveland Clinic with the first of two explosions when an exposed light bulb came too close to x-ray film, igniting the film.

One-hundred and twenty-three people lost their lives in the fire or from the poisonous gas coming from the x-ray film. Most of the dead were patients and visitors.

But that particular fire was probably far from Philanthropist Francis Drury's thoughts when he built his home on Euclid Avenue 17 years earlier. He made more than a million selling his Perfection Stoves between 1905 and 1915. Between, he built the 34-room Tudor home, nicknamed Drury Mansion. He lived there until 1924 when he sold the home. He was gone by the time the fire at the Cleveland Clinic happened along the same road. Others had moved in and out. Then in 1972, the Drury Mansion was leased to the Ohio Adult Parole Authority as a halfway house for paroled convicts.

It was right away that some of the inmates complained about the windows closing and the doors banging shut when no one was there. Staff heard groaning and footsteps. Then the inmates began seeing the ghostly form of a woman with long, black hair and wearing a hospital bracelet. She would appear, then burst into flames. Fingers pointed to the fire at the hospital bringing this woman to haunt those within the mansion.

The home is now privately owned. Whether the new owners hear or see the ghost is unknown. However, the stories linger still, mostly around Halloween and in the archives of strange happenings in Cleveland's historic homes.

Prospect Street
Cleveland, Ohio 44115

Cuyahoga County

A True Disbeliever

Even non-believers fall prey to a haunting once in a while. They tend to laugh it off as a bad dream and assure those who heard their shriek of fear that they weren't scared at all and perhaps just caught off-guard. They make a point of letting everyone know they weren't drunk the moment a full-bodied apparition crossed their path or threw them from their beds. It was probably just coincidence. Or was it? A man from Cleveland laughed his experience off. But he could never quite account for the strange occurrence.—

An apartment on a busy Cleveland street in 1886 became the focus of a ghost story for a man who didn't believe in ghosts.

AN OHIO GHOST STORY

Experience of a Young Man With an Apparition.

Thrown From Bed At a Very Early Hour In the Morning by Some Unseen Agency. A Strange Coincidence—

Cleveland O., January 10,— About 3 o'clock last Friday morning Mrs. Emily Frayne, a widow, of Hamilton, Ont. , who had come to Cleveland to visit her sister who resided in a block on Prospect street died very suddenly.

Frank Lamb, a fresco painter, aged 33, who occupies apartments adjoining those in which Mrs. Frayne died relates a remarkable story. He says "Between 2 and 3 o'clock on the morning in question he was awakened by something and looking across the room he saw a lady sitting on a lounge about four feet from the bed. 'What do you want?' he asked. Raising her right hand, the lady said: "Hush, hush!" and then she disappeared.

Lamb is a disbeliever in ghosts, and he at once made a search of the room and examined the lock of the door. He found that the door was securely fastened, and getting into bed, he lay for ten minutes thinking about the strange occurrence. Suddenly the clothing on his bed and the tick were tumbled off by some unseen power, and he found himself on the floor.

Being angry by this time. Lamb made another search of the room without finding anybody. He then opened the door and as he did so Mrs. Hodden, sister of Mrs. Frayne, came from her room into the hall saying: "My sister is dead." Lamb declares that he was not excited, and that he was perfectly sober. He cannot account for this strange occurrence. Other people in the block who heard Lamb fall also left their rooms, and they corroborate his story as to the coincidence with Mrs. Frayne' s death. The coroner has decided that the woman's death was caused by heart disease—

Butte City, Mo - Jan 11, 1886

Cleveland Big Four Railway Union Freight Depot

1010 Front Avene
Cleveland, Ohio 44113
41.501169,-81.704605

Cuyahoga County

Big Four Railway Ghost

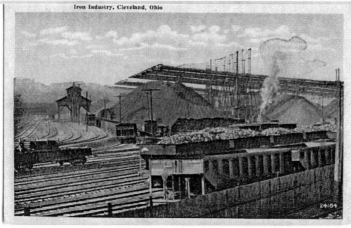

Iron Industry, Cleveland, Ohio

The Cleveland, Cincinnati, Chicago and St. Louis Railway, also known as the Big Four, had over 4600 miles of track through Illinois, Indiana, Michigan and Ohio by 1925. One major area it passed through was alongside the Lake Erie shoreline of Cleveland where it had its Union Freight Depot near the mouth of the Cuyahoga River. On the opposite side of the river, the Pennsylvania Railroad's Cleveland Ore Docks were located on a peninsula called Whiskey Island.

It was here, along the mouth of the Cuyahoga River, the two industries would unite in a ghost story where an ore dock worker returned from the dead to haunt those working in the Union Freight Depot only months after his death.

MANGLED, LIES HELPLESS -Dock Worker Has Legs Taken Off by Train and is Found by Passer By. George Ferencz, thirty-two, living at 700 Minkon-av., S.E. lost both legs in an accident yesterday morning on the B. & O. railroad near the Superior-av. Viaduct. Ferencz was on his way to his work at the Pennsylvania ore docks, when he was run down by a train. The train crew apparently did not know of the accident, for he was left lying on the track until found some time later by another man passing on his way to work. Saxton's ambulance was called and the injured man taken unconscious to German hospital. Both legs had to be amputated, one below the knee and the other above the knee. Owing to the stupor in which Ferencz lay it was not until last night that his name could be learned. The doctors believe he will recover. . .

Cleveland Plain Dealer. December 6, 1909. Mangled. Lies Helpless. Historical Archives

Railway tracks where the ghostly wails of the ore worker were heard. Tracks zigzagged and wove their way from inner city to the industries along the waterfront areas like Whiskey Island where the ore docks were found. Workers walked the train tracks often to get to their jobs. Some tracks, like those above twisted and turned making it nearly impossible to see a train coming until too late.

He did not recover. Instead Ferencz died the next day and was buried in Calvary Cemetery. But workers at the Union Freight Depot believed his spirit lingered near the place he was killed; his last moans heard long after his body was settled comfortably seven feet under the ground.

Those working at the Big Four Railroad along the Lake Erie shoreline and police who were called in heard the groans at midnight, regardless of weather or noise that should have rendered the ghost unseen or unheard.

Declare 'Spook' Echoes Cry of Workman Killed Near Freighthouse.

Big Four railroad employees stationed in the vicinity of the Front-st. crossing have been getting goose flesh, losing sleep, taking nerve medicine and trembling over terrifying humanlike moans which rend the midnight air every Sunday in that locality.

The uncanny wails, Michael Weir, flagman at Front-st,, says have been causing him no end of uneasiness for the past two months. Joe Domley, night watchman, at the freighthouse has been carrying a bigger stick since the moaning, as he calls it, first became apparent and Miss May Murphy, night telephone operator in the freighthouse declares she has been thrown into hysterics on more than one occasion by the uncanny sounds, which seem to have no permanent place of origin.

Jess Millard and Frank Kennedy of the Lake Shore police say they have tried for weeks to unearth the mystery, which is growing on the nerves of many, but all efforts to locate the genesis of this nocturnal phenomenon have been baffled.

Those who heard the spooklike groans say they resemble those of a human being in death agony. They bob up first from one place and then another. It appears from the descriptions given to come from the spirit of some restless person, who in life could not stand still long enough to get a check cashed. In fair and foul weather, above the noise of grinding wheels upon heavy rails, it is said, the sound comes regularly and punctually about midnight.

Those who keep accurate track of such things declare the ghost of an ore handler, who was run over and killed at this spot Sunday night, Dec. 6, last, is haunting the place.

Cleveland Plain Dealer. February 14, 1910. p. 1 CUYAHOGA COUNTY. Declare 'Spook' Echoes Cry of Workman Killed Near Freighthouse. Historical Archives

Where the Union Freight Depot once stood and ghostly wails were heard.

Grays Armory

1234 Bolivar Road
Cleveland, Ohio 44115
41.498958,-81.681795

Cuyahoga County

Grays Armory

The 'Cleveland Grays' were originally founded as a private volunteer militia in 1837. They took their name for the gray color of their uniforms. Although their initial purpose was to defend the city and aid local law enforcement, the militia also fought in the Civil War, Spanish American War and World War I.

After utilizing several different facilities in their first fifty-five years of service, they built a five-story, castle-like armory in 1893. Nowadays, the building, called Grays Armory, is used for parties and special events. It has a ballroom, shooting area and historical memorabilia. But the past still comes alive . . . or at least partially so. People hear footsteps in the building that do not come from the feet of the living. Ghostly apparitions of men dressed in Civil War uniform have appeared and disappeared before human eyes.

Old River Street
Cleveland, Ohio 44113
41.499104,-81.70409

Cuyahoga County

Death Follows "The Black Lady"

Those living in Cleveland in the early 1900s loved a good ghost story. And the Plain Dealer never left their customers unhappy when it came to printing interesting articles about the gruesome, chilling and even the funny side of scary. Quite often, tucked into special sections of the newspaper were attention-grabbing tales of ghostly phenomenon that would even tantalize the most skeptic spook critic.

In fact, in 1909 when a strange and dark apparition began appearing to a local lady and folks around her began to die each time she saw it, a reporter was sent to interview her for a story.

And here, is what he found . . .

DEATH FOLLOWS "THE BLACK LADY." Mrs. Mary Corley Says She Has Seen a Strange Apparition. Her Father Passed Away Soon After the "Ghost's" First Visit. The Figure Came Again And her Husband Left the World. Who is "The Black Lady?" That is the question which worries Mrs. Mary Corley, who lives at No. 22 Old River street.

"The Black Lady" is an omen of death to Mrs. Corley. In short, the "apparition" to which Mrs. Corley gives the above appellation is described as a woman who looks into the window of the Corley home on River street. The "woman" looks through the window for an instant and then disappears. Twice within a month Mrs. Corley has seen the "apparition." Each time the appearance of the figure was followed by a death. Mrs. Corley's father, Patrick Riley, was a brother of Councilman Riley. Patrick Riley died on Sept. 16, about ten days after Mrs. Corley avers she saw "The Black Lady" looking into her window. Nov. 7 Mrs. Corley again saw the "apparition" at the window. Three days later Mrs. Corley's husband, who was apparently in good health was taken suddenly sick and died.

Each time Mrs. Corley saw "the Black Lady" she threw up her hands and screamed and she fell in a faint.

A section of old River Road today.

Mrs. Corley is unable to explain the strange phenomena according to the story she told a friend. The features of the "apparition," or whatever it may be, can be plainly seen by Mrs. Corley, although she cannot remember the face as resembling that of any friend who has died. On each occasion the figure appeared at the same window of her home on Old River street. The window opens into a sitting room which is now but little used on account of this fact. Mrs. Corley is deathly afraid of "The Black Lady," and would not go into the room alone for the world. The figure is described as being dressed in solid black and always in the same costume. A hood is worn over the head and her eyes are black and piercing in their intensity. ⟹

Mrs. Corley says the figure has a sallow complexion, so pronounced as to give the figure a deathlike appearance. The "woman" looks into the window and the moment Mrs. Corley looks in that direction it disappears. . .

Patrick Riley, who died Sept. 16, left an estate of about $50,000. Last summer he took his daughter, Mrs. Corley, to Europe. They returned early in September. A few days after their return Mrs. Corley claims she saw "The Black Lady" looking into the window. She went to a well known undertaker who is a friend of the family and told him, it is said, that he would soon be needed by the family.

"Why?" asked the undertaker.

"I've seen 'The Black Lady,'" replied Mrs. Corley.

At that time Patrick Riley was apparently in good health. About a week later he was taken suddenly ill and died in a few days. Nov. 7 Mrs. Corley sent for the undertaker to settle up some business matters.

"I suppose you will be needed again soon," said Mrs. Corley to the undertaker.

In response to a question Mrs. Corley replied: "I have seen 'The Black Lady' again." At that time Mrs. Corley's husband was enjoying good health. Three days later he died.

Mrs. Corley is not naturally superstitious. She is a strong, healthy woman, about thirty years of age. She enjoys robust health. A Plain Dealer reporter called on Mrs. Corley last evening at the home of her uncle. Councilman M. Riley, on Washington street. Miss Riley, a daughter of the Councilman Riley and a teacher in the Detroit street school, received the newspaper man and upon learning his errand immediately declared the family did not want any newspaper notoriety. She also said she nor her family believed that Mrs. Corley saw any apparition at all and that the figure was a creature of Mrs. Corley's imagination.

"It's all due to her nerves," said Miss Riley. "Such things don't bother me, because I never had any nerves."

Mrs. Corley was finally persuaded to come into the room, but she firmly refused to discuss the matter at all. She declared that she did not care to have the matter get into the newspapers. She did not deny that she had seen the figure, which she called "The Black Lady," but she refused to say anything about the matter. . .

Cleveland Plain Dealer. December 1, 1899. Death Follows The Black Lady. Historical Archives

The Lake View Cemetery
12316 Euclid Avenue
Cleveland, Ohio 44106
41.514233,-81.598648

Cuyahoga County

Presidential Wanderer

It is hard to imagine 107,500 burials in one single graveyard, but Lake View Cemetery in Cleveland encompasses almost 283 acres of interments with nine miles of roads and more than a few historical notables tucked inside its gates. The memorial and burial of the 172 children and two teachers who died in the Collinwood School fire on March 4, 1908 is here. John D. Rockefeller, founder of Standard Oil is buried at the cemetery. Eliot Ness, who brought Al Capone to justice has his ashes scattered within. Even a US president, James Garfield has his resting place in Lake View. In fact, among the ghosts that are supposed to haunt Lake View Cemetery, James Garfield is probably the most prominent. The 20th president of the United States, he was sworn in less than a year when he was shot and killed. He has been seen wandering the graves by his monument.

Agora Theatre And Ballroom

5000 Euclid Avenue
Cleveland, Ohio 44103
41.503981,-81.653976

Cuyahoga County

Raincoat Man

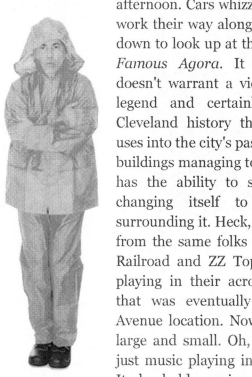

It is quiet along Euclid Avenue in the afternoon. Cars whizz pass and a few bicyclists work their way along the pavement. Few slow down to look up at the sign that states: *World Famous Agora*. It isn't that the building doesn't warrant a view. It is somewhat of a legend and certainly an iconic piece of Cleveland history that blends its numerous uses into the city's past. It, like many of the old buildings managing to avoid the wrecking ball, has the ability to survive by molding and changing itself to fit the pop culture surrounding it. Heck, it was purchased in 1985 from the same folks who helped Grand Funk Railroad and ZZ Top gain prominence after playing in their across-town concert theatre that was eventually moved to this Euclid Avenue location. Now it is rented for events, large and small. Oh, and by the way, it isn't just music playing in this landmark building. It also holds a raincoat-clad ghost making its dramatic debut once in a while. The **Agora Theater is haunted by this spirit that has been seen on both the stage and the catwalk.**

The Agora actually opened in March of 1913 as the elegant Metropolitan, hosting opera, musical comedy, orchestral events and theatre. By 1932, it had styled itself into The Gayety with the venue of vaudeville/burlesque. By the mid-1940s, the theatre was once again showing dramatic acts and then continued on as a movie house. For a while, it was called the Bijou Theatre. From 1951 to 1978, Cleveland's pioneer radio station, WHK had its

studios located here and the building was known as the WHK Auditorium. It lay vacant for a while. It would later become the Cleveland Grande, the Disastrodome and the New Hippodrome Theatre.

That's a good thing for the city, tucking a little bit of history underneath its belt. And it is a good thing for the ghost that haunts the hallways and the stage. It has a place to endure too. But who is this ghost and where did it come from? Dressed in a raincoat, it seems to show up at the oddest times and fade away into nothing at all. Who it is, remains a mystery. It could be any of the figures from The Agora's eclectic past—a vaudeville actor, a radio show host, a burlesque show guest or even someone coming to watch a concert. But one thing we do know— he must have been trying to get out of the rain!

Erie Street Cemetery
2254 East 9th Street
Cleveland, Ohio 44115
41.497039,-81.683654

Cuyahoga County

Eerie —Erie Street Cemetery

It is less than 9 acres, holds over 8,800 bodies and was purchased for one dollar in 1825. *It* is the Erie Street Cemetery and is also Cleveland's oldest existing cemetery.

Photo Courtesy: Michael L. Sekeres.
Erie Cemetery is Cleveland's oldest public cemetery. Before the land for it was purchased, an impromptu lot on the N.E. corner of Ontario and Prospect was used. But as the city crept up on its gates, those within were moved to the Erie Cemetery grounds.

The Erie Cemetery holds in its grasp some of the earliest settlers to the city. It was almost lost to road development when a politician came up with the idea of a horse-drawn streetcar turnaround right through the middle of the cemetery in 1920.The public fought to keep Erie Street Cemetery where it belonged and they won.

There are 168 veterans buried there from the American Revolution through the Spanish American War. Cleveland's first European settlers, Lorenzo and Rebecca Carter and members of their family are buried here. Five men are buried in a communal grave after they were tragically killed in a waterworks tunnel explosion in 1901 during the construction of a clean water project. And there are four babies from the Aaroe family in the late 1800s who never made it past infancy.

Those are just a handful of the many people stuffed into this old cemetery. There are two American Indians buried in Erie Cemetery, too. One is said to haunt the grounds — Joc-O-Sot, a chief of the Sauk. He fought against the U.S. in the Black Hawk War, but later was a fishing guide along the lake shore and also travelled the US and abroad performing theatrical shows.

Ghosts still walk the grounds both night and day. I took this shot with an infrared camera while walking the cemetery grounds in the early afternoon. A shadowy figure kept darting just out of the corner of my eyes. Later, looking at the image, I found two ghostly men lounging near the corner of a gate beneath a tree where no one had been. A third ghostly man is also in the second tree.

Jac-O-Sot, an American Indian who became a part of the early community, is buried in Erie Cemetery. However, legend states he did not want to be buried here at all. In fact, he was so angry after death, he made the ground shake hard enough, his headstone was shattered. Oh, and his ghost walks the cemetery still.

Joc-O-Sot died at the age of 34 in 1844 and wanted to be buried in the northern part of the US. Instead, Jac-O-Sot got stuck being buried in Cleveland. Jac-O-Sot is one of the ghosts roaming the cemetery. He's still a little angry about getting trapped in there for eternity, so he walks the hard-packed soil and is seen sometimes as a shadowy figure darting around. There is a legend that Jac-O-Sot was angry he was buried at Erie Cemetery and he made the earth shake so much his gravestone broke. A new marker replaces the old, but you can still see the shattered stone behind it.

Erie Cemetery is open dawn to dusk and is quiet during the day. Take a walk in it and you might also see some of the shadowy figures running around Erie Cemetery too. And maybe you'll be greeted by the early settlers of the city or the ghost of a Sauk chief who might take his irritation out on you of being buried away from home.

Franklin Castle
4308 Franklin Boulevard
Cleveland, Ohio 44113
41.485656,-81.716521

Cuyahoga County

Dead Babies in the Walls, Bones and a Murdered Servant Girl

The famous Lady in Black is said to peer out of the upper windows.

Franklin Castle is haunted. People see stuff inside the old mansion Clevelanders claim is Ohio's most haunted house. It was big enough news that the Sunday January 19th, 1975 Zanesville Recorder printed an article: *Human Bones Found Inside Haunted Mansion.* It appeared Sam Muscatello, the owner at the time, found the femur or thigh bones along with part of a pelvis within a wall he was excavating to make a passageway for the guided tours he gave at the four-story, 20 bedroom mansion.

Dr. Lester Adelson, county coroner, confirmed the bones were certainly human, although he could not identify the age, race or sex. The doctor was able to state, though, the person was 65 to 67 inches. It did not say in the newspaper if Dr. Adelson had any remarks on Sam Muscatello's statement that at one time, Mister Muscatello had seen a shadowy light flash out of the very room he had been working in. Then, he watched as 'this thing' came down the stairs before it passed right through him.

But others have known the Franklin Castle was haunted long before the newspaper article ran. It was always claimed by those in the suburban neighborhood there was something odd

The Tiedemann House—aka Franklin Castle

going on in the home the Cuyahoga County Auditor lists as built in 1864 by a German immigrant, Hannes Tiedemann.

It wasn't like everything didn't fall into place to make it a haunted house. In a relatively short period of time, four children and an adult perished in the huge home. There were rumors more than just the Tiedemann children died on the property—hearsay flew that babies were born at the home and when they died, their bodies were hidden in walls. Oh, and it was said Hannes Tiedemann murdered a young servant girl in a fit of jealous rage on her wedding day. She was then placed in a hidden passageway where she rotted away. Now she lingers as a lady in black who weeps at the top of some stairway. *They* said not long before Hannes, himself, would pass away, he sold the house to a German Socialist Party— Nazis— who met and discussed espionage and who had a doctor among them who operated on more babies and hid their mutilated bones in the walls. It was whispered forty of the Nazis were caught by local police and executed in a shootout in the home.

Franklin Castle is haunted. Michael Devinko who owned the home in 1985 believed it was. He told local newspapers there was poltergeist activity when he lived there. And there probably is. But it isn't from a mad murderer or a Nazi activist or a servant girl who is trying to find her way out of the walls. It is probably haunted by the spirits of a family who once lived there, happily or unhappily going about their daily lives or reliving the normal tragedies families went through in the later 1800s.

To set the story straight—**Actually, Hannes Tiedemann (1832-1908) did exist. He was a Prussian-born immigrant who, after initially farming in northern Ohio, moved to Cleveland with his sister and her husband in 1855. Over the following years, he married another Prussian-born immigrant, Luise (1837-1895), and became a wholesale grocer with the firm Wiedeman and Tiedemann. In 1864, Hannes and Luise had their first child, August, and in 1865, a second child was born who they named Emma. As with many couples starting a family, there also comes a new home. So on October 6, 1865, they moved to a house owned by Alonzo Wolverton on what is now 4308 Franklin Avenue—where Franklin Castle now stands.**

Although the family lived continuously at the address from 1866 to 1895, the present gothic mansion was not erected until 1881 on the property. It was during the time the Tiedemanns lived in the homes on Franklin Avenue that they suffered the loss of three infant children in the family along with the teenage Emma. Each of these deaths were from diseases common in the era and now would, most likely, be eradicated by modern medical procedures and drugs. Ernst was born in 1869 and died at six months of age from meningitis (brain fever). Wilhelmine was just over two months when she passed away in 1871 and Albert was only two months old in 1873 when he died. In January of 1881, Emma died at the age of 15 years from complications of diabetes. All are buried at the Riverside Cemetery family plot. Of the six children, two—Dora (1871-1906) and August (1864 - 1906) — lived to adulthood.

Franklin Castle was eventually sold to the Mulhauser family in 1897 and then, went through several other hands. Some saw ghosts, others, like the Mulhausers didn't.

From 1921 to 1968, it was the home for German ethnic cultural organizations and singing groups.

If there were supernatural booms and bangs around the old mansion when they were using it for events, no tales have been told. In fact, the haunting stories did not begin until the mid-sixties. The James Romano family moved into the castle for a short period and there were different reports about ghostly children roaming the building and strange mists forming inside the walls.

Reverend Tim Swope of the Universal Christian Church began building a place of worship at Franklin Castle in the 1970s. He told The Mansfield News Journal in the June 8, 1976 newspaper that the third floor of the building would stay about ten degrees cooler than the rest of the house. He also stated that Karen, a ghost in the home who had been murdered by hanging there, would touch people on the neck.

Since then, it has changed hands several times. It depends upon the owner whether ghostly hands touch them, strange mists appear or spirits are roaming the rooms and halls. But the house *looks* haunted. It has the flair of an old castle and people still drive past slowly, looking for whoever walks the halls. They probably don't care if the ghosts are spies from old wars or poor servant girls murdered in a fit of passion. It doesn't really matter if the hand that might reach out and touch them or the eyes that stare at them from the windows is a young woman who died from a disease or a dead newborn baby stuck inside a wall. They just want to see stuff, see *something*, be scared. And perhaps, they will.

Old Crawford Property And Long Gone Shanty of Rosa Colvin

Private

Along Schady Road Olmsted, Ohio 44138

Cuyahoga

Tragedy in Olmsted Falls

Road to Olmsted where cabin was tucked into the woods.

Olmsted Falls. The name hardly reeks of thieves, ne'er-do-wells, a murder mystery and an ensuing ghost story. It resonates more like a small town woodland retreat with waterfalls and wandering streams, a paradise for those living within.   Perhaps it is a delightful area now and was also an ideal place to raise children back in the 1800s for most. But for one person during the chilly spring of 1866 while winter was still boasting a bit of wet snow in northern Ohio and the Civil War was just a few steps away from the past, it was more like a living hell. A murder was committed and it had more than a few scandalous characters fitting the bill of a good whodunit detective novel. Oh, and it ended up having a ghost, too.

The ghoulish little mystery would begin on the cold morning of Wednesday March 28, 1866 for most of the good, newspaper-reading citizens living in and around the quiet hamlet of Olmsted, about 17 miles southwest of Cleveland proper. Upon picking up the Cleveland Daily Leader, the tantalizing headline written in bold, black letters would tickle their sense of macabre and gruesome. ***OLMSTED FALLS MURDER. Body of Mrs. Colvin Found. Her Head More Frightful than Medusa—***

OLMSTED FALLS MURDER. *Body of Mrs. Colvin Found.*
Her Head More Frightful than Medusa
McConnell Not Found, Dead or Alive
THE MYSTERY DEEPENS *A Visit to the Slaughter-Cabin.*
EXAMINATION OF PRISONERS.

*The body was found twenty-six rods south of the cabin, between a log and pile of wood, which had been toppled over upon the corpse. A man stepped on a blood-saturated dress east of the house. His boot-heel crimsoned the snow at the next step. The direction was thus guessed, and the body quickly found. The removal of the first stick revealed the feet. The clothes were hitched up about the chest, exposing the body. The corpse was removed to the Falls, and exhibited as found. The head was turned to the right or twisted that the hand rested on the cheek. The eyelids were open, but the eyes held no fire and shed no light. The upper teeth protruded upon the lower lips. The hair was disheveled and clotted with blood. A blow with the butt axe upon the top of the head had torn off the scalp, exposing a triangular space of the fractured skull large as one's palm. The top of the left ear was cut off, and the ear-ring dangled in her gory hair. The other ring lay on the floor, and a broach in a water-pail. The expression of the face was inexpressibly horrible. The corpse was dressed, when found, in a checked merino gown of reddish color. In the pocket were a pair of cotton gloves and a horn-handled three-bladed knife. . . **Cleveland Daily Leader., March 28, 1866. OLMSTED FALLS MURDER.***

The shabby Colvin shanty, now long gone, was described to appear much like the cabin above.

The shack-like hovel of a cabin where the murder victim was found was rented by William Colvin and his wife, Rosa. They had a boarder of three weeks, a drifter by the name of Alexander McConnell. Both Colvin and McConnell were working as woodcutters on the lot the cabin was located and for the Robert Crawford family who had a contract for furnishing wood to different parties in the region.

The cabin was described in the Cleveland Daily Leader as:

". . . *the shanty of Colvin, a hovel, twenty feet by eighteen in dimensions, and constructed of rough boards was situated in the center of a small clearing. To the west, east and south lay a thousand acres of forest, while woods on the north shut out the view of the few houses of the neighborhood. Fifty rods east stood a barn, the only building in sight. There was no hint of yard or garden. The open area was inexpressibly dreary, and the house seemed the picture of all that is wretched, dismal and profane in life. But no conception of the squalor could be formed until the interior was inspected. There were but two rooms, lighted by one common and two very small sized windows. No more were needed, since daylight flooded the house through the wide cracks between the upright boards. The floor was loose and full of fissures and chasms. In the front room were a bed, table, a broken cooking stove, two or three chairs, a cupboard in which were dirty dishes, bread and crackers, besides several barrels, boxes, etc A few comic pictures were pinned like a naturalist's insects to the siding . . ."* **Cleveland daily leader., March 28, 1866. Olmsted Falls Murder.**

It was the landowner, 28 year-old Robert Crawford who, upon stopping in at his barns on his property near the shanty cabin early Sunday morning of March 25th, was hailed by William Colvin and invited inside. Most likely, Crawford was a little uneasy about entering the cabin. He had fired William Colvin from his job as a woodcutter for "laziness" within the past few days. The boarder Alexander McConnell, too, had allegedly quit because the work was too difficult.

Upon entering, Crawford immediately noted with alarm pools of blood on the floor. He also observed two men present- William Colvin and an acquaintance, Joseph Miller who were cooking breakfast. Rosa Colvin and the boarder, Alexander McConnell, were not present. Both men appeared surprised at the scene pointed out by Crawford and denied seeing the blood pooled on the floor until that point. Nor had they noted 'gore' saturated on a mop and delicate bloody fingerprints on a broken window, doorknob and walls. There was a mark of a head in blood in two places on the wall and an axe covered in blood was found near a ladder leading to the loft on the second floor.

The constable was called and the two men, William Colvin and Joseph Miller, were detained by neighbors including 21 year-old Michael Eglar. When asked about overlooking the seemingly obvious signs of violent struggle, William Colvin stated he had not come home until after dark. In fact, he had gone to Berea to look for work in the quarries along with the boarder, Alexander McConnell, about 6 miles away. Both men were looking for lighter work than chopping wood. Colvin was also searching for a new place to board. Although Rosa had started to follow him, Colvin sent her home. Not long after and near the Cleveland and

Olmsted Falls Depot and Tracks.

Toledo railway tracks, McConnell complained of knee pain and turned back toward the shanty too.

Later, Colvin had met up with Joseph Miller and the two returned after dark (between 7 and 8 o'clock at night). The door was locked and they had to force their way in. It had been snowing, a light amount still lying on the ground. The men did not turn on a lantern. Instead they napped, ate a small supper, then sat by the fire and talked through the night. They had not noticed the blood without any light. William Colvin stated he figured that his wife had run off with McConnell and it was the reason neither had returned. However, he did find that some clothing was missing including a pair of pantaloons, a pair of boots, a pair of shoes, a coat end vest, and trousers. Within a short amount of time, the body of Rosa Colvin was found carefully concealed between a log and a pile of wood. It was thought, surely, that the body of Alexander McConnell would also be found. Neighbors, Mary Eglar and William Busby, had seen both Rosa Colvin and Alexander McConnell going toward the home. McConnell was carrying a satchel in his hands and a roll of clothing under his arm. Rumors flew that the two were having a torrid affair and when William Colvin had returned the evening before, he had caught them in some act. Others stated that perhaps McConnell plundered the home and Rosa Colvin caught him in the act.

It became apparent, they must find Alexander McConnell, either alive or dead. Regardless, the facts about the victims and the suspects that were known were this:

Suspect:

Alexander McConnell, was described as a thickset man of about five feet five inches, with brown hair. He was 35 or 36 years-old and a farmer hailing 19 years earlier from Ireland and father of nine children, six of those from his wife's previous marriage. At a later trial, the reporter for the Cleveland Daily Leader gave this descriptions of his appearance: " . . . *He is thirty-five years of age; considerably below the medium height, has brown hair; blue eyes; with a low forehead, narrow at the top. He is not very neatly dressed, and has anything but a prepossessing appearance.*"

He had come to Ohio via Ottawa, Canada for far less respectable reasons than he would testify to the judge. McConnell clearly stated he owed a man $12.00 and was trying to find work to pay him back before he was sued. He does not elaborate in his confession that it was over the sale of a horse, and McConnell also fractured the man's skull during an ensuing quarrel. He found work about 4 miles from Olmsted Falls chopping wood on the property of Robert Crawford and had boarded with Rosa and William Colvin for a little over three weeks. He was last seen at eleven o'clock on Saturday, March 24th with a satchel in hand.

Suspect:

William Colvin, who was nicknamed "Stuttering Bill", was about forty years-old and had been described as lazy. He had only been in Ohio two years, moving often and about every one to two years. When taken into custody on March 28, 1866 the reporter from the Cleveland Daily Leader portrayed him as "*a Scotchman and about forty years old. He has a swarthy complexion and looks like a black snake. The eye is impenetrable and perfectly devilish. And this suits his nature . . .*" He was described in court by witnesses as a wife-beater, liar and whiskey drinker.

When neighbors visited his home on March 25th, he was found wearing a vest and drawers with blood on it as if he had dragged a body. He excused his bloodied clothing stating he had carried in a side of beef from buckboard to house. Blood was found pooled near a window at his home along with a broken window.

When Rosa was alive, the Crawford shanty her husband rented was surrounded by thick woodland. Now, it is farmland and homes.

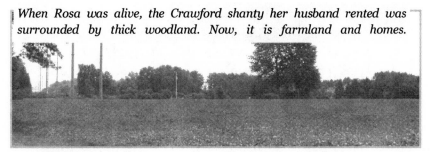

Suspect:

Joseph Miller was in the home with William Colvin the morning the body was discovered. He was described as "*a pumpkiny-looking youth with fuzz on face and apparently, a brain of mush.*" He appeared to others as sluggish and apathetic, a follower and slow-witted.

The Victim:

Rosa Colvin was about 37 years-old. Little is said about her except the day she was murdered, she was wearing a calico dress that was red in color. She must have liked jewelry because the day they found her body, amongst the puddles of blood on the floor, they found an earring in a pail and a bracelet on the floor. She had been seen with bruises on her face at times before. She had one child who had died and she kept the child's clothing in a trunk beside her bed along with $150.00 that would be missing when she was found dead.

The mystery came to a head when Sheriff Nicola used a bit of common sense, and traced back the whereabouts of the drifter, Alexander McConnell. Alexander McConnell, a suspected murderer of Mrs. Colvin, was captured in Ottawa, Canada by a John Dell, a detective engaged by Sheriff Nicola. The suspect was wearing a pair of trousers stained with blood, admittedly belonging to William Colvin.

ARREST OF MCCONNELL

Everything now depended on the finding McConnell, dead or alive, and every effort to that end was put forth. Should he be found, nothing could save Colvin and Miller from conviction. Sheriff Nicola became early convinced that the real criminal was McConnell but where to find him? By the merest accident the place of McConnell's residence became known, and John Odell, a shrewd detective in the employ of the Revenue Department of this district, was dispatched to Ottawa, and succeeded in arresting McConnell at his home Fitzroy about thirty miles from that city. In his possession was found Colvin's overcoat, fine boots, quarry boots and pants. Besides these things a watch and about $150 money was missing. There could be no doubt of McConnell's guilt, for the goods in his possession and his manner when arrest showed it.

Cleveland daily leader., August 11, 1866 details. ARREST OF MCCONNELL

Alexander McConnell would confess on the fateful day of Saturday, March 24th 1866 he had actually stolen William Colvin's clothing including a pair of pants, overcoat and two sets of boots. He headed for the railroad on his way to Elyria, but accidently ran into Rosa Colvin. Rosa saw the clothing and confronted McConnell stating he was stealing them, but McConnell stated he was merely meeting her husband, taking the clothing to him because they were heading to Cleveland. Unbelieving, Rosa stated she would tag along to meet her husband, but McConnell convinced her to return home to the shanty with him and await William Colvin's return.

After both returned to the Colvin cabin, McConnell admitted he had stolen the clothing and that he was leaving. Rosa grabbed up a fireplace poker in her hands, refusing to allow him to leave by placing herself in front of the door. McConnell began to push through and Rosa hit him with the poker. Enraged, McConnell struck her with his fist, knocked her to the ground. A fight ensued and McConnell finally grabbed up an axe and struck her in the head. She was killed instantly. McConnell was hanged for his crime.

Her life may have been taken from her, but her spirit remained at the cabin. The Miller family, who boarded there after the Colvins, were visited nightly by the strange sound of an axe banging against wood and the sound of furniture being shoved around.

Veritable Haunted House.—A gentleman from Olmstead says that there is such a thing as a "haunted house"; and that the shanty occupied by William Colvin, in which Rosa Colvin was murdered, now occupied by a family named Miller, is nightly visited with strange, unearthly noises moving of furniture, and creating the wildest consternation in the dwellers, and the greatest curiosity in the neighborhood.

Cleveland Daily Leader., August 13, 1866 Veritable Haunted House

The Old Bancroft Farm in Chagrin Falls

Cuyahoga County

Strange Manifestations in Chagrin Falls

The Gorge below the Falls.   CHAGRIN FALLS, Ohio.

VILLAGERS WROUGHT UP OVER STRANGE MANIFESTATIONS IN A FARMHOUSE. *Cleveland, O., Sept. 4 The village of Chagrin Falls is wrought up over the strange manifestations in the farmhouse of Henry Bancroft. Mr. Bancroft is 75 years old, and a well-respected resident of the village. Beginning with Wednesday morning articles in his home began to catch fire, apparently from nothing, and to burn violently. Napkins, socks, aprons, towels and the like suddenly flare up and are consumed. This happens only in the day time. Mrs. Bancroft's dress caught fire while on her. Opinion is divided as between the supernatural and the belief that some evil-minded person is making use of a chemical compound to annoy the Bancrofts.* **Marietta Daily Leader September 6, 1897. Buckeye News. Fire Spooks. New and Interesting Happenings Within Our Borders.**

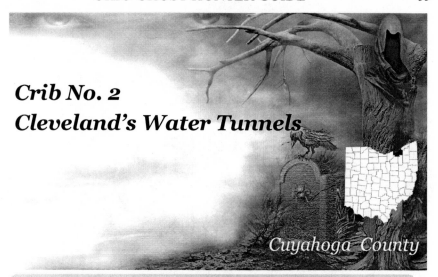

Crib No. 2
Cleveland's Water Tunnels

Cuyahoga County

A Watery Grave—Ghost of Cleveland's Water Tunnels

Tunnel construction scene in East Side Lake tunnel circa. 1900. Courtesy: Library of Congress.

Waterwork intake tunnels were built out into Lake Erie to pipe in fresh water for public use in Cleveland as early as 1856. At the same time, much of the sewage water was also being pumped back out into Lake Erie and close to these intake tunnels. So much so, the city began building tunnels farther out into the lake due to the amount of pollution near the shoreline.

Working in the tunnels was dangerous. In fact, six disasters occurred during its construction from 1898 to 1916 killing 58 men. It shouldn't be surprising, then, a ghost began to show up to send more than a few workers into a frenzy.

Working in the tunnels. Courtesy: Library of Congress.

CRIB FIRE COST NINE LIVES

One Tunnel Employe Met His Death While Attempting to Save a Fellow Workman. . . Nine men lost their lives yesterday in the most frightful disaster that has ever happened in the vicinity of Cleveland, the burning of the temporary waterworks crib No. 2. Five were burned to death in the fiery furnace of the blazing crib. Three, who took refuge in the lake, were unable to maintain their hold on the wreckage to which they clung for safety. Their scorched and battered hands lost their grip and they sank beneath the water as their luckier comrades were being rescued by the tug Sprankle and a yawlboat from the barge Wilheim. Twenty-two men were picked up from the water and taken ashore.

NOBLE RESCUER PERISHED.

The black horror of the catastrophe was partly relieved by the thrilling rescue of nine men entombed in the waterworks tunnel, 136 feet below the burning crib. In this work, Plummer Jones, a volunteer, lost his life after performing a series of feats of the greatest heroism . . . Cleveland Plain Dealer, Aug 15, 1901. CRIB FIRE COST NINE LIVES. Historical Archives

On August 4th, 1901 cinders from a boiler stack were ignited starting a fire in a temporary crib built as quarters for workers. Three men were drowned and five burned to death.

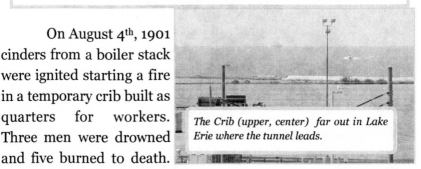

The Crib (upper, center) far out in Lake Erie where the tunnel leads.

A ninth man died trying to save the lives of those within. His name was Plummer Jones.

It would be Plummer Jones whose ghost came back to haunt the tunnels in January of 1902. Many men would leave their jobs because of the spirit they would see within the darkened walls.

SAW A "GHOST" IN THE TUNNEL. CRIB WORKMEN DECLARE THEY ARE HAUNTED BY AN APPARITION. THREE SCARED MEN THROW UP THEIR JOBS AND HURRY FOR SHORE

The fact leaked out yesterday that a supposed apparition in the tunnel at crib No. 2 threatens to seriously interfere with the progress of the work there. Digging under air pressure recommenced four days ago and already four men have thrown up their jobs and come ashore, either frankly declaring that they had seen the supposed ghost or giving various pretexts to the bosses and confessing to their comrades that they were afraid to again enter the tunnel.

The tunnel foremen and officials of the waterworks department in charge of the tunnel work laugh at the story. They have done their best to kill the absurd superstition by ridicule. The workmen are ready enough to laugh with them over the ghost joke while they are above ground and to vow that no spirit can have power to frighten them, but once in the dimly lighted tunnel with the stories of last summer's horror, in which so many men lost their lives, fresh in their minds, they are more credulous.

Most of the workmen, however, while they admit that there is something queer about the tunnel, say that they will continue to work there in spite of any supernatural influences that may be at work. It has been the weaker men whose nerves are less strong than those of the typical tunnel digger, who have hurried ashore with their baggage during the past week.

J.E. McCarthy, a "skinner" or mule driver, was the first man to see the "ghost." He had been employed for a long time as a waiter at crib No. 3. He decided at last that he would prefer the job of driving the mule through the shaft at the other crib, as something that would be easier work at better wages.

Last Thursday night he went down to his first shift. The men went behind the air lock to work. McCarthy and the mule waited in the empty tunnel, 3,000 feet from the foot of the shaft. McCarthy is twenty-one years old, a steady workman of good physique and apparently not subject to nervous attacks. He sat composedly in the tunnel watching the rows of electric lights down the long vista of masonry walls and waited for the time to drive the mule car out with the load. . . ⟹

. . . A half hour passed and the elevator man at the top of the shaft was startled by the sudden shriek of the signal whistle for his machine. Such a blast had not been blown on the crib since the fatal night of last summer, when the men hemmed in by the flames tried to signal to the shore for aid. The cage was sent down the shaft at its top speed. The trembling operator waited above expecting a horror but unable to imagine what had gone wrong. When the cage appeared McCarthy was its only occupant. He was pale with fright, and the operator says his hair stood straight up on his head.

"I have seen Plummer Jones," he gasped. McCarthy had left his mule and run from his station to the foot of the shaft, a good half mile. He insisted on waking Foreman Van Duesen and telling his story to him. The time was 2:30 p.m. and Van Duesen's reception of the ghost story was the most vigorous blessing that such an apparition ever received.

But McCarthy had had enough. He wanted to go ashore at once and if that was not possible to go ashore on the first boat. He said that nothing could induce him to enter that tunnel again. He came ashore the next day on one of the tugs that reached the crib.

Three more workmen came ashore yesterday, who had thrown up their jobs. The workmen on the crib speak of the ghost as the "man with the whiskers" and he is a regular feature in the life there at present. The men have little to enliven their leisure hours and the tunnel "ghost" is the joke with the least superstitious. The others laugh, but uneasily.

Cleveland Plain January 19, 1902: p. 10 SAW A "GHOST" IN THE TUNNEL.

Regardless of the ghostly return of Plummer Jones, enough men stayed on to finish the intake tunnel that would provide fresh water to Cleveland even today. Three more tunnel disasters occurred after the 1901 event during construction of the tunnel, six in total with 58 deaths. Perhaps, Mister Jones knew his rescue efforts were still not complete when he died. He had returned to warn the workers of what was to come. And perhaps, he is still there wandering within the dark and slimy wet walls waiting. . .

Old Village of Newburg, Ohio 44105

Cuyahoga County

SAY GHOST HAUNTS PLACE

SAY GHOST HAUNTS PLACE

Neighbors Near Scene of Murder and Suicide Declare Weird Being Walks There.

Still brooding over fancied wrongs, neighbors say that Peter Pandek of Newburg, who shot and killed his wife as she clasped her baby in her arms, then sent a bullet into his own brain on the morning of July 28, haunts the vicinity of the tragedy.

People who live in the neighborhood claim to have seen the weird form near the place of the shooting. They say that the wraith swings a revolver and threatens those who come near.

A number of families have moved out of the neighborhood.

Cleveland Plain Dealer, Historical August 17, 1908. Say Ghost Haunts Place. Historical Archives

Old Central Police Station

Cuyahoga County

Central Police Station Ghost

Was it a ghost or something less mysterious frightening those within the walls of the old Central Police Station in 1905? You make the call —

SPOOK, BANSHEE OR MURDERER? CENTRAL STATION POLICE HAVE MYSTERY WITHIN THEIR OWN WALLS.

RIGID INVESTIGATION BEING CONDUCTED BY BEST OF THE FORCE.

There is a deep, dark and impenetrable mystery at Cleveland's central police station, and the best talent of the department is now occupied in an attempt to solve it. It may be murder; it may be ghosts. Which, it remains for the police to learn, and the efforts to unravel the problem will be unceasing until every separate thread lies exposed to the departmental view.

At one end of the first floor corridor in the station is a little side room. Upon the doors are the cabalistic letters "Reporters' Room," and within, upon the floor, are scattered papers and cigar stubs, and things. The chairs and tables are much frequented by the familiars of police headquarters. There are also many cats in the neighborhood of the station; but that, of course, has nothing to do with the present tale. . . ⟹

The old Central Police Station in Cleveland, Ohio. *Courtesy: Cleveland State University, Cleveland Memory Project*

Late yesterday afternoon, for once in a year, the room was deserted. The doors were closed, and an air of quiet wafted gently about the halls. A squad of policemen entered to report, and breathed deep signs of relief as they noted the deserted atmosphere round about that little room.

"Ain't it great?" said they.

Suddenly came a sound.

"Wo-o-o-w."

Loud and long it wailed, its cadence floating up the stairway to the court in progress on the second floor.

"What's that," said the squad, halting.

"Wow, Whack, scr-a-a-sh, we-o-o-w."

"It's murder. That's what it is," said the squad with conviction. "Send for Toy Marshal."

The squad was re-enforced by other detachments from the officers' room downstairs and the attachés of the chief's and captains' quarters. With commendable decision a sergeant took charge and deployed his men.

"Guard those doors well," he thundered. "Let no guilty man escape. Hold guns in readiness. Three men deploy and look through the jail windows and find out what you can see."

The jail windows look directly into the little room, and the officers at once deployed.

They returned with blanched faces.

"C-c-cant s-see anything," they gasped. "It's sperrits."

"Whack, zim-m-m me-eow," came from the beleaguered room.

Then up dashed a volunteer. Trained in many a fight, learned in the ways of ghosts and murderers, he rashly promised to storm the room and rescue the unhappy victim of assassin or banshee. . . ⟹

As the now great force of patrolmen stood back, arms to readiness, he stealthily slipped up to the door. Slowly, softly he turned the knob and opened a narrow crack. He looked in. He opened the crack a little wider.

"They ain't nothin' here," said he.

As the officers rushed pell mell into the benewspapered and cigar stubbed apartment, two lithe shadows glided among their feet, unseen, and departed. The room was empty.

Now the police are investigating the mystery. Who was it made that noise? What ghost invaded central station, or what murderer dared pursue his nefarious course within its walls? What did he do with the body? These questions will have to be answered, for the best talent of the department is at work, and soon the whole nefarious thing will be laid open to public horror. In the meantime, unconnected with the mystery and inconsequent to this story, "Siss," the station cat, has a very sore ear, torn, it is believed, in combat . She is being cared for in the turnkey's room.

Cleveland Plain Dealer January 29 1905: p. 16 SPOOK, BANSHEE OR MURDERER?
Historical Archives.

Near Portland- Outhwaite Rec Center

237 Outhwaite Avenue

Cleveland, Ohio 44104

near 41.490311, -81.653235

Cuyahoga County

Grewsome Ghost Story on Outhwaite Avenue

In 1902, The St. Paul Globe featured a special story in the Society section about a home in Cleveland, Ohio that centered around a ghostly girl in brown appearing to a local woman at her home on Outhwaite Avenue. The homes along this section of early 1900s Cleveland are now gone—a recreation center and housing have replaced them. Even if the buildings once lining the street can only be seen on old maps tugged from a dusty shelf, maybe the ghosts still linger. And if you're lucky and driving along these roads going home from work or simply traveling through, perhaps you might still see them.

GOBLINS IN COLORS Ghosts in Cleveland Haunted House Do Not Appear in White Garb QUITE NEW GHOST STORY

Instances Recorded by the Psychical Research Society in Which the Eidolons of the Departed Revealed Themselves.

Special to The Globe. CLEVELAND, Ohio. July 5.—A grewsome ghost story has just come to light in this city which has led to a family named Taubert—vacating then-residence on Outhwaite avenue. It incidentally serves to revive the flagging interest in ghosts and to remind us that none of the historic ghost yarns about English historic places have been raked up a la coronation. . . ⇒

Cleveland, unlike some old English towns and castles, boasts no antiquity and has hitherto scarcely considered itself in the spook belt.

Hence the alarm which has seized upon its inhabitants now that a genuine ghost has appeared and the trepidation of real estate dealers lest a development of the industry should take place to the disturbance of values.

The Taubert domicile, which now has been vacated in favor of its eerie occupants, is a two-story cottage, with a gable over the street and a small front porch, at 237 Outhwaite street, its former residents having been William Taubert, his wife, a baby and Mrs. Minor, the mother of Mrs. Taubert.

Mrs. Tauberts story is a straight-forward and circumstantial account of what she saw, which led her to move precipitately.

"We are alone at night," said Mrs. Taubert, as my husband is on night duty. On a certain night recently I was suddenly awakened from a sound sleep by rappings on the walls such as I never heard anything like before. The noises came first from one direction and then from another and I became so frightened that finally the baby awoke and I determined to get up and sit in a chair all night. I turned the lamp up so that it burned brightly. While I sat at the table the light grew suddenly dim and I saw a young woman, dressed in brown, standing in the middle of the room. There was no way by which she could have entered as I was sitting close to the door and between it and the figure. Just as I had recovered from my surprise and was about to speak to her the woman disappeared, seeming to pass clear through the floor. . . ⟹

Knocking Is Kept Up.

"All the time that the woman was in the room the knocking kept up, but it ceased when she disappeared."

A remarkable story paralleling the foregoing was told by Mrs. Minor. She said:

"I was sitting in the room adjoining the bedroom and Mrs. Taubert had gone in to attend to the baby who was restless. As I looked in I saw a man dressed in black standing by the bed in the corner. My daughter could not see him and when I looked in again he had gone. I would not sleep in that house again for anything you might offer.

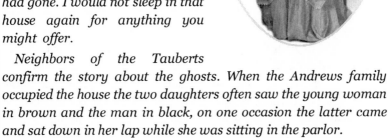

Neighbors of the Tauberts confirm the story about the ghosts. When the Andrews family occupied the house the two daughters often saw the young woman in brown and the man in black, on one occasion the latter came and sat down in her lap while she was sitting in the parlor.

The following extracts from the reports of the Society of Psychical Research of London relate similar cases of ghost seeing which have been duly authenticated. The only thing necessary now is for some scientist to discover a method of securing these aura or essences, whichever they may be, for exhibition in our museums where as scientific curiosities, they might prove both interesting and educational.

A lady whose account was corroborated tell the following remarkable story. *"One night on retiring to my bedroom about 11 o'clock, I thought I heard a peculiar moaning sound, and some one sobbing as if in great distress of mind. I listened very attentively and it still continued; so I raised the gas in my bedroom, and then went to the landing window, threw the blind aside—and there on the grass was a very beautiful young girl in a kneeling posture before a soldier, in a general's uniform sobbing and clasping her hands together, entreating for pardon; but, alas! he only waved her away from him. . .* ⇨

Figures Quickly Disappear.

"So much did I feel for the girl that without a moment's hesitation I ran down the staircase to the door opening upon the lawn, and begged, her to come in and tell her sorrow. The figures then disappeared! Not in the least nervous did I feel then; went again to my bedroom, took a sheet of writing paper and wrote down what I had seen. It appears the story is only too true. The youngest daughter of this very old, proud family had had an illegitimate child; and her parents and relatives would not recognize her again and she died broken hearted. The soldier was a near relative (also a connection of my husband's); and it was in vain she tried to gain— the soldier's —forgiveness. So vivid was my remembrance of the features of the soldier that some months after the occurrence when I happened to be calling with my husband at a house where there was a portrait of him, I stepped before it and said: "Why, look. There is the general!" And sure enough it was.

Here is another from the report of the Psychical Research society:

"On a certain evening in March I was dressing myself to go to a dinner party at Admiralty house, Vittoriosa Malta. I had accepted Admiral and Mrs.'s invitation, much against my will, as a dear friend was lying seriously ill at Brighton. However, the latest account had been so cheering and hopeful that I had allowed myself to be persuaded by my husband into going. An eerie feeling was creeping over me in an unaccountable manner, but I tried to throw it off, and succeed to a certain extent; still, something made me turn my head around and stare into my husband's dressing room, which opened into mine.

I distinctly saw a hand waving backward and forward twice. I rushed into the room— it was empty.

Soon afterward my husband came up stairs, and I told him what I had seen, but he put it down to 'nerves.' ⟹

Public housing off Outhwaite Avenue today somewhere near the location the haunted home stood. And the ghosts haunted.

An Unusual Prayer.

. . ."*As we crossed the water the cool night air seemed to revive me, and I began to laugh at myself for letting my imagination play such tricks. We got home somehow, and I dragged myself to my room and commenced undressing. While taking down my hair I distinctly felt a hand pass over my head and neck, as if some one was assisting me. I told my husband— to be laughed at. I knelt down to say my prayers. Instead of praying (as I had been used to do) for God to make my friend well, I, without any will of my own, prayed that he might be taken out of his misery. I went to bed. Something came and lay beside me, I clung to my husband, who tried to calm me assuring me that there was nothing to hurt or frighten me. A cold mouth seemed to freeze on my cheek, and I distinctly heard, "Good-by, Sis, good-by," in my friend's well known voice. Still my husband declared he could hear nothing. I said 'I am sure Mr . Abbott is dead.' My husband said I was hysterical and overwrought drew me toward him, and held my hand till I fell asleep—for I suppose it was a dream and not a vision I had. Be this as it may, I saw my friend come into my room; a livid mark was across his face, was dressed in a nightshirt and his feet were bare. He came and sat beside me— told me he was dead— that be had left me some money and before he died had wished to make some alteration in his bequest, but the end had come so soon he had not the time to do so. He repeated his 'good-by,' kissed me and disappeared.*"

"*I told my husband of my dream and marked the date. Five days afterward a letter with a deep black border came to me from my friend's brother telling me his brother had passed away at 10 o'clock, March 13. Allowing for the difference of time, Mr. Abbot must have come to me either just before or just after his death. The legacy left me was as he had stated, also the fact that he intended to make a change as regarded it, but though the lawyer was sent for, he came too late.*"

The Saint Paul Globe., July 06, 1902. GOBLINS IN COLORS

Detroit Court
Cleveland, Ohio 44102

Cuyahoga County

Cleveland's Haunted House

CLEVELAND'S HAUNTED HOUSE

Mysterious Rappings Puzzle the Police Put on Guard—Spooks Rap on Demand   *The upper part of the dwelling house at 18 Detroit Court, Cleveland, O, the lower part of which is occupied by Arthur Cox and family, is haunted by uncanny ghosts or spirits, according to stories earnestly told by the family and also by several policemen. At 11:20 Saturday night the family were startled by a series of strange knocks or rappings on the wall upstairs. They investigated, but found no one. The noises continued and the frightened inmates made a hasty exit to the street and notified the eighth precinct police station.*

Sergt. Washington and several patrolmen were sent to investigate. They found the upstairs unoccupied, but the rappings on the wall continued in their presence. The loud knockings traveled all over the room. Patrolman O'Loughlin started to keep time with his foot on the floor. The officers were surprised by the spirit answering. "Rap in the center of the ceiling," shouted Patrolman Carey. The jovial spook immediately complied. It is also claimed by the police officers and the Cox family that when the ghost was asked to knock 10, 15, 20 or 100 times, it cheerfully responded. The police remained on guard till four o'clock in the morning, the strange sounds ceased.

The officers laughed at the strangeness of the affair, but are unable to explain it, except by saying: "We seem to be up against the real thing." The entire neighborhood is nervous, and the police are on guard.   **The Lima News. November 9, 1899 Clevelands Haunted House**

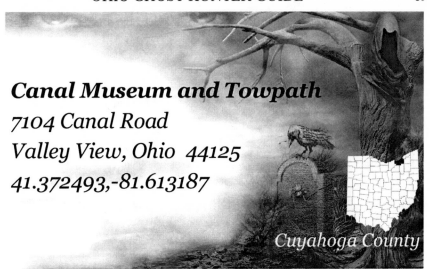

Canal Museum and Towpath
7104 Canal Road
Valley View, Ohio 44125
41.372493,-81.613187

Cuyahoga County

Hell's Half Acre

Hell's Half Acre, Circa 1875.
Photo Courtesy: Michael Schwartz Library, Cleveland State University.

Now it is the Canal Visitor Center and museum, a part of the Cuyahoga Valley National Park Service. Visitors walking or biking along the towpath trail can stop in and get a hands-on history lesson about the canal from friendly, smiling staff. But stopping in at this particular establishment hasn't always been so wholesome. At one time, it had earned the nickname: Hell's Half Acre. And along with it, there are a few ghosts left behind.

It all started when the Ohio & Erie Canal was built between 1825 and 1832. It travelled 308 miles through lift locks and along its watery trail from Cleveland to Portsmouth, Ohio. Along the routes, inns, taverns and general stores popped up to

cater to the needs of those working and traveling the canals.

Hell's Half Acre—Modern View

The section along Lock 38 in Valley View, Ohio has a building often misidentified as a lock tender home. Actually, it was created as a general store and home. The first half was built in 1827 and another section built in 1850. The building was partially used as an inn and tavern, serving a rowdy crowd of canal workers frequenting the bar for prostitutes and alcohol. Over the years, it was also used as a general store, dance hall and even a bootlegging establishment. Eventually its unsavory reputation earned this little place the name of Hell's Half Acre.

It has also earned another less than savory reputation—that of being haunted. Ghosts from the tavern's past like to show they still are there. Knocks, bangs and voices have been heard inside the building. Two lovers—a young Union soldier and his sweetheart— are also said to walk opposites sides of the canal, never to meet. They appear near the visitor center for just a moment, then disappear from sight.

Terra Vista Cemetery
(aka: Tinkers Creek)
11505 Tinkers Creek Road
Valley View, Ohio 44125
41.36697,-81.60634

Cuyahoga County

Old Ghosts of Pilgerruh

It has gone through more than a few names: Tinker's Creek, Old Indian Cemetery (it abuts an Indian burial mound), Hillside Cemetery, and Terra Vista. But it is Pilgerruh, meaning "Pilgrim's Rest," which is the most catching to the ear and tongue. And yes, it best describes its origin. The cemetery holds a few old pioneers of early times.

On March 19, 1813 Lieut. Caleb Baldwin was laid to rest here. He died on his return from the army March 9. He was only 24 years-old. But his stone isn't the oldest one there. There's Captain Peter Comstock who died in 1803. There are folks buried there who lived into the 90s and little ones who died before they were one year old. Their stones have withstood the test of time—wind, snow, rain and vandalism. And ghosts. It has a few that visit from time to time. Children's giggles and voices have been heard here. A ghostly shadow walks among the graves. You can walk there too. Visitors can park at the abandoned road. It is a short hike up a hill to reach the flat uplands of Terra Vista.

Paines Hollow
The Old Lerman Farm
Paine Road
Painesville, Ohio 44077

Lake County

The Ghost of Paines Hollow

There was a ghost in Paines Hollow. The exact place is about a

A road near Paines Hollow where the ghostly story began. . . and ended.

forty minute drive from downtown Cleveland and about 1/4 mile from Paines Fall Park and on property that Frank Lerman once owned. It is gone, now, the ghost. At least that was the information printed in papers all across the U.S. at the time which were the late days of the summer of 1922. The moment the sheriff ordered the body buried, the ghost faded away not only in history, but also from the farm it had been haunting for 7 long years.

The August 13, 1922 Ogden Standard Examiner newspaper out of Utah began chronicling the story with a bold banner stating: ***GHOST LEADS MAN TO BODY IN WELL***.

The October 14, 1922 Hamilton Evening Journal had a small note concluding the entire event. It simply stated: *Second Degree is Charge for Lerman*. But what happened between is best explained below by the Friday October 20, 1922 Hamilton Evening Journal:

GHOST PLAYS PART *In Murder Trial Now On In* ***Painesville*** *WHITE VAPOR HOVERED OVER WELL WHERE BODY OF SLAIN MAN WAS FOUND.—Painesville, Oh. Oct 20—*

Lake County people are watching the trail of Frank Lerman of Cleveland, in local courts, on a charge of second degree murder with interest perhaps unrivaled in the history of the county. By it, they recall to mind an incident that will, they say, become a part of the community's legendary history—the ghost of Paines Hollow.

An abandoned well, a secluded farm and the usual grisly details that go to make up the background for a ghost story enter into the events that led up to the arrest of Lerman. The story starts seven years ago, when Lerman owned a farm at Paines Hollow. At that time, Harry Lipenstick, handyman on the farm, suddenly disappeared. Farmers wondered what had become of the young man, but his presence soon was forgotten. Years passed, and in that time, owners of the farm were many. The crops became poor, and finally Carl Logies of Cleveland purchased it. Logies asserted that night after night, about 9:30, as he approached the barn where he kept his cattle, he saw "something white" slip past it.

He said the mysterious thing always disappeared in the direction of the well, and gradually he claims conviction came upon him that the well had something to do with the mystery.

One night in bed, he said he heard his dog barking outside of the house. Then, according to him, the animal's bark changed to a whine of terror. Logies said he rushed outside, and as he looked past the dog to the well on the other side of the road, he saw the white mist hovering it. Then it disappeared and the dog quieted down.

Logies said he finally could stand it no longer, and early in July of this year, he started to clean the well out. For years it had been filled with large rocks. As he started to pull the stones and debris out, Logies claims he had a premonition he was on the right track. . . ⇨

. . . *At a depth of 20 feet, he found a half-rotted shoe, containing the foot bones and nails of a man. He immediately called Sheriff Spink and when the county officials arrived, the well was cleaned out. In the bottom was found the decomposed mass of what had been a man. A watch—with a peculiar ruby charm, identified the body as that of Lipenstick. The watch was set at 9:35.*

About the body was three heavy straps, and the skull was shattered and flattened. Lermans' arrest followed a day later, an hour after the body of Lipenstick was laid to rest in an unmarked grave in the cemetery here.

Lerman was indicted by the Lake County grand jury on a charge of second degree murder. The hour at which the watch of the dead man stopped is pointed to significantly as the hour at which the spirit is supposed to have roved around. Since the body has been buried, farmers claim the spirit of Paines Hollow is at rest.

Hamilton Evening Journal Hamilton Ohio - Friday October 20, 1922 - GHOST PLAYS PART In Murder Trial Now On In Painesville WHITE VAPOR HOVERED OVER WELL WHERE BODY OF SLAIN MAN WAS FOUND.

The property has changed hands over the years. The ghost was said to never return. The spirit now at rest. Still, perhaps, you must wonder if once in a while Lipenstick doesn't wander from the cemetery to visit his last resting place.

Lake Erie College

391 W Washington Street

Painesville, Ohio 44077

41.718046,-81.254071

Lake County

Lake Erie College

Lake Erie College is a private college founded in 1856, and was originally developed as a women's college. It is now coed, opening its doors to not only women and men but also, we hear, ghosts. A ghost named Stephanie, haunts College Hall. Her face has been seen in the fourth floor windows. And Helen Morley makes a grand spectral entrance in a white flowing dress at the music hall.

Lake Erie College —about 1908. Courtesy: Columbus Metropolitan Library Collection

Fairport Harbor Lighthouse

129 Second Street

Fairport Harbor, Ohio 44077

41.757451,-81.277782

Lighthouse Ghost

Lake County

With a melodious name like Fairport Harbor, you wouldn't think there would be any bloodcurdling ghosties or goulies creeping up out of the Lake Erie waters into this small town. The town is as peaceful and cozy as the name implies. Of course, isn't that always the case for every horror movie playing out along a coastline? You have a pretty, little village with friendly people and a snug little harbor to boot, and in comes a fog or zombies or some other spirit to shake things up a bit.

Well, Fairport Harbor may have a ghost. But it isn't going to do much more than give you a gentle startling while you peruse the lighthouse and museum. It seems the thing creeping around in the dark is smaller than you might think. During the early half of the nineteenth century, 120 miles of southern shoreline of Lake Erie attracted settlers making their way to Ohio, Michigan, Wisconsin and other states. One of the places many of the cargo ships stopped for restocking was the busy Fairport Harbor along the mouth of the Grand River.

The Fairport Harbor Lighthouse was built on the west pier out of bricks in 1825 to guard this gateway of new opportunities along the coast. Samuel Butler was the first keeper of Fairport Harbor Lighthouse and was an active abolitionist. Not only was it a safety harbor for those ships traveling along the shoreline, it also provided sanctuary for slaves making their way to Canada before and during the civil war. But, by 1868, the lighthouse was falling into ruin. It was rebuilt in 1870.

It was not until August of 1871, when Captain Joseph Babcock came to be head keeper of the lighthouse, the ghost story comes to life. During this time of Captain Joseph Babcock's term, his wife and family kept several cats in the living quarters which is now the museum. Missus Babcock was ill for some time and found great comfort in the presence of her cats. For years, volunteers and curators at the museum have seen what they described as a ghostly cat playing in the museum. Whether others believed the story or not, it was difficult to deny there might be some truth—during the installation of a new air conditioning system, the mummified remains of a cat was discovered between the walls. For how long it has been there, remains a mystery. It is believed to be one of the cats from the previous residents of the lighthouse!

Not every lighthouse can boast they have the mummified remains of their ghost! Nor can most museums offer a trip up to the top of a lighthouse. But sure enough, Fairport Harbor Lighthouse has both tour-guided and self-guided tours, a museum *and* their little ghost ready for viewing. It is a sure-hit with the kids. . . and adults too and it has a great historical museum of lighthouses with unique items not seen elsewhere. And it is only a short walk to the beach and park.

You simply have to visit the lighthouse to meet the ghostly resident. You will be amazed.

Rider's Inn
792 Mentor Avenue
Painesville, Ohio 44077
41.713052,-81.260119

Lake County

Greetings from a Ghost

Rider's Inn was a stagecoach/traveler's stop along the Buffalo, New York and Cleveland route providing food and lodging for the night. Joseph Rider, his wife, Suzanne and their family ran the inn from 1812 to 1902. During this time, the owners also took in fugitive slaves heading toward Canada and seeking a safe haven along the Underground  Railroad route. During the Civil War years, soldiers were given a place to stay on their way home.

In 1902, George Randall bought the Rider's Inn, added a restaurant addition before utilizing the property as a speakeasy during the prohibition years. From 1940 until 1979, the Lutz brothers owned the property. Elaine Crane and her mother eventually purchased the inn. You can still get a taste of the past at Rider's Inn. It is now a bed and breakfast with a pub and restaurant. You may also get to meet a few visitors from long-ago. The Rider's Inn is said to be haunted by Suzanne Rider who still greets guests with the same type of hospitality offered two-hundred years ago. She has been seen at the front door and on the upper floors.

Swift Mansion -
Light and Hope Orphanage
52374 Gore Orphanage Road
Amherst, Ohio 44001
41.355052, -82.335234
  And—Andress/Gore Orphanage Cemetery
  10799 Gore Orphanage Road
  Amherst, Ohio 44001
  41.336697,-82.331519
    Lorain County

The Legend of Gore Orphanage

People have seen ghosts among the lush layer of poison ivy and tangled mire of brush at the sparse remains of Gore Orphanage in a remote area near State Route 60 in Lorain County, Ohio. They hear ghostly steps on the large slabs of stone from the front porch. There are sounds coming from the floor still laying nestled beneath the thick green canopy of trees and nearly hidden by cornfields and forests from the roadway.

Screams bang off a raggedy stone wall. They hover over an old well made of flat creek stones. A gate post lingers amongst the forest growth and the aged limbs and branches that fell from the trees during the winds of winter and early spring. There are other echoes of the past atrocities, too, heard in screams and even a haunting sing-song voice belting out a child's nursery rhyme. Because it was here Old Man Gore, the rickety cruel man who ran

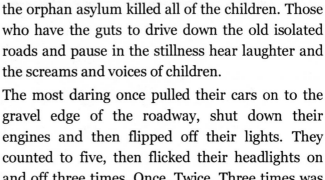

the orphan asylum killed all of the children. Those who have the guts to drive down the old isolated roads and pause in the stillness hear laughter and the screams and voices of children.

The most daring once pulled their cars on to the gravel edge of the roadway, shut down their engines and then flipped off their lights. They counted to five, then flicked their headlights on and off three times. Once. Twice. Three times was the charm to sit in the darkness and the silence and just. . . wait. It was then, they would hear the pitiful, dying screams of orphans who had been locked into their rooms on that cold, dark night by Old Man Gore. It is said, most dare seekers were not disappointed.

But even before they drove cars to Gore Orphanage, they came in carriages as early as a hundred years ago to listen to the legends, hear the screams, see Old Man Gore trudge up through the woods with an ax in his hand. They came to see the ghosts of orphan children in tattered clothing and latch on to the worst thing that could happen to a child—abuse and murder by one who should have been holding them, hugging them, giving them tender kisses on the forehead before bedtime prayers. Because one night, tired of their cries, Old Man Gore lit a match, caught the place on fire. The children, all of them, went up with the house in a fiery explosion. But that is not all. That was the end to the tragedy. Here is the beginning: there *was* a Swift family who built the mansion there and two of their children died. The Wilber family who came after fared no better.

Four of their grandchildren lost their lives to disease. Their ghosts wander the house, peek from trees, laugh at those who walk the paths around their old abode. Why wouldn't they? Their parents hosted elaborate séances at the mansion after they died and tried to bring them back. Bad luck, it would seem, started the whole mess with the orphanage in the first place. Because the land is cursed. If you take a stone or a stick or even an old brick with you as a souvenir to remind you how adventurousand daring you were for visiting the orphanage, you will certainly have something hideous happen to you.

The Swift Mansion—They fondly named it Rosedale.

It is the stuff that makes utterly great and horrid ghost stories — innocence lost, sad-eyed orphans trying desperately to flee a burning building, an evil old man and a horrifying way to die. There was death from disease and abandoned burials lost to time. And cursed land. The land just off Gore Orphanage Road has it all. And it is probably the reason the story has been perpetuated for a century, building upon itself, rising, falling, but never completely going away. Because surely there is truth to it, isn't there? Perhaps, there is. Johnathon Swift really owned the property in the early 1800s. A wealthy farmer in New England, he was deeded a homestead grant of 150 acres of land for his service to the country as a veteran of the War of 1812. In 1818, he married Elizabeth Root and began building a promising future in farming.

He came to the small hollow nestled in the hills, built a cabin and began clearing the land. His farm grew along with his home and a family with six children as years passed. There was one loss, though, at an early date. Swift's five year old daughter, Tryphenia, died at age five in 1831. By 1840 to 1842, he was able to build a substantial sized home in what was called Swift's Hollow. The price was exorbitant for the times at $5000.00.

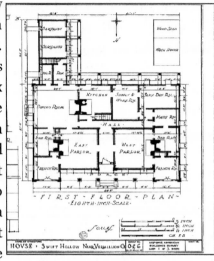

His home, compared to a Greek temple, had fourteen rooms including two front rooms, six fireplaces, a basement kitchen, servant's quarters, servant's dining room and French-style windows and doorframes. Four marble decorative columns were shipped from New York by boat and an oxcart. The property surrounding it was well-manicured and professionally landscaped with ornaments. To top it all off, Johnathon Swift fondly named it 'Rosedale'. Times were good at the estate, then his son, Heman, died in 1849 at age 24.   By 1865 and due to poor investments, the Swifts sold their property to Nicholas and Henrietta Wilber, Lumber Dealers from New York.

5 year old Tryphenia (Feb. 5, 1831) and 24 year old Heman (Sept 26, 1849) died while they lived at Swift Mansion. They are buried at the Andress Cemetery on Gore Orphanage Road.

The new owners shared the home for some time with their son, Miller, and his wife, Harriet. For nearly 35 years, the family lived in the home, not a small amount of time.

There was always talk amongst the townspeople the Wilbers were spiritualists along with family friend, Dr. Hudson Tuttle of Berlin. Odds are, this could be true. It was not something new at this time, nor a crime, even if many small town folks were superstitious of such things. In fact, during the mid-1800s it became quite a craze, performing séances in 'home circles' and trying to speak to the dead.

Tragedy struck in the early 1890s. Between January 13th and 19th, 1893, four of Nicholas Wilber's grandchildren (Miller's children) died of diphtheria when an epidemic swept across Ohio. All four children were buried next to each other at nearby Maple Grove Cemetery Jesse, age 11; May, age 9; and twins Roy and Ruby, age 2 1/2. They did *not* die at the home and instead in Berlin, Ohio. They were hastily buried in Maple Grove Cemetery because of the chance of spreading the disease.

Nicholas lived there until his death in February of 1901 and the home was sold to the Sutton family. It stood vacant for several years and became, even then, known as the Haunted House of Gore. It was at this point some historians believe the ghost stories began, entwined with the tragic fire at Lake View Elementary in Collinwood, near Cleveland which was about 60 miles away. The horrific fire took the lives of 172 children, two teachers, and one rescuer and shocked the nation.

On March 4, 1908, a steam pipe in the Lake View Elementary School's basement caused a wooden floor above it to overheat. Within a short time, the entire school went up into a blaze with no time for many of the students to escape. The Newark Advocate described it as this: - *The Greatest Calamity In The History of American Schools - One Hundred and Sixty-Five little Tots are Devoured by Hungry Flames —Newark Girl a Victim Scenes of Horror That Beggar Description—Parents Compelled to Stand Helpless While Little Ones Die Before Their Eyes.*

But the Swift Mansion, although vacant, was still very much present. It caught the eye of Reverend John Sprunger, wealthy industrialist and builder, and his wife, Katie, who upon the death of their child, resolved themselves to mission work. Sprunger had started the Light and Hope Missionary Society in 1893

School for Girls

and a print shop, publishing company and orphanage near Cleveland. Around 1903, Sprunger purchased the nearby Hughes farm along with three other neighboring farms including the Howard's farm and buildings to house the children. The boys

Home for Boys

lived at the Hughes farm and the girls were housed at the old Howard farm. The workers lived at the old Swift Mansion.

It was here they established the Light and Hope Orphanage that would eventually encompass over 500 acres and hopefully, become a self-sufficient farm and home for the children. It would be the old Swift mansion that would provide a boarding area for the many workers and assistants at the orphanage. The farm had separate dormitories for boys and girls at the top of the hill by the river, a chapel, school house, buggy shed and print shop for the *Light and Hope* publication.

A 1910 U.S. census shows there were 45 people living on the property including 27 children, Katie and John Sprunger and 15 helpers and assistants. Sources state there could have been up to 125 children cared for on the property at a single time. From the onset, the orphanage was plagued by complaints and investigations of abuse and slave labor at the farms. Beatings were a common form of punishment to the children and they were rented out to local farmers as workers. They labored at the farm and complained they were not allowed schooling. Accounts from the children stated it was an unhappy life, many were beaten and the food was poor.

Renting orphans out to other farms was not uncommon in the past to help ends meet.

It was breaking news in the Vermillion Telegram in September of 1909 when former children from the orphanage testified: "I have been beaten and seen other boys beaten with a strap in the hand of hired men or the preacher, and the food we had to eat was often spoiled . . ." It was also stated the children found bedbugs, rats and lice in their beds commonly and on one occasion, the children were forced to eat a cow that had lay dead in a pasture. Leftover heads, livers and lungs of cattle were purchased as food quite often for the children. Prayer, alone at times, was used as a means to heal the children instead of medicines. An underground railway to help children escape was even started in Vermilion in 1909.

Underground Railway Led From Orphanage to Vermilion Homes - Women of Vermillion Helped Youngsters To Escape Through Sympathy - Three women who have befriended children who have run away, labored for the welfare of the place until they discovered how the children were treated, then they adopted for methods to take children from the home. One of the women who has a little boy in her possession says that she told several of the boys how to escape from the place and just how to get to Vermilion, and that she advised them that she would leave the door of her home open to them night and day. . . **The Evening Telegram - ELRYIA, OHIO SATURDAY SEPTEMBER 4, 1909 - Underground Orphanage Led from Orphanage to Vermillion Homes**

But the orphanage did stay open even after Sprunger's death in September of 1911. It was not closed until July of 1916 and was purchased by real estate investors not long after. Pelham Hooker Blossom of Cleveland purchased the Orphanage property. He leased it out to local farmers, then finally sold the land.

The Swift home was burned down in December of 1923. It was surmised homeless people had taken up residence there, caught the place on fire. Now, the only things that remain are old foundation stones, slabs of rock and an old gate/hitching post. The old home where the orphanage was has a new house in its place. And still, the ghost stories linger. It does not seem to matter Old Man Gore never burned up the place with orphans inside. People still smell smoke there at night. They say tiny, bloody footprints have been seen in the snow. There was always the frightening image of Old Man Sprunger chasing around little children with a stick to beat them. No one seems to mind that nothing really remains but the old gate post to lead the adventurous back to the spot. There is something fun about searching out those treasures of the past that dead people once saw too. Besides, bad things happened to little children here, at least that's what the children said, that's what those who tried to save them said.

People did die here—the two Swift children who are buried in the Gore Orphanage/Andress family Cemetery. There are probably a few settlers who died here even earlier than them. Perhaps Sprunger died here, too. At least one little orphan boy died nearby, 'coasting' on the back of a car. And those old, disturbing memories still linger of cruelty on the property to sad little orphans who may have returned to the place to haunt Old Man Sprunger and his hired hands for their wrongs. And there have been tales of a ghost child swinging on an old tree. Maybe. It is worth the hike beneath the trees to check it out, find the old well, imagine what it looked like before it was burnt to the ground. Some put a little baby powder on the back of their car to see the tiny baby footprints show up in the powdery residue. Try it. Maybe, you'll see the ghost of someone's past like thousands before you. Because, they say they have.

There never was a Gore Orphanage. Gore Orphanage was really Light and Hope Orphanage. Traditionally, 'gores' were the result of errors during land surveying when towns were laid out. It was an area between two adjoining towns that was technically not belonging to either. Such is the case with the 'Gore' in the original Gore Road. It was a small section of land between Lorain, Erie and Huron Counties mistakenly surveyed long ago. It was eventually added to Lorain County.

On a late afternoon ghost investigation, we did catch an EVP of a little girl saying "Tryphenia" when asked who was at the home and a very clear "Get off of me." The image of a little girl peering out from behind a tree appeared in a photograph.

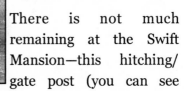

There is not much remaining at the Swift Mansion—this hitching/gate post (you can see where it was in relation to the house in the image above on the right hand side of the home), slabs of rock, rock walls and a well. The property is now a part of Lorain County Metroparks. You can contact them for the current times the park is open to the public at: 12882 Diagonal Road | LaGrange, Ohio 44050.

Phone: 1-800-LCM-PARK.

Interesting historical information from a collection provided by Dan Brady: http://danielebrady.blogspot.com.

Crybaby Bridge
52299 Twp Hwy 34
Vermilion, Ohio 44089
41.360009,-82.334296

Lorain County

Crybaby Bridge

Just past Swift Mansion, a bridge crosses the Vermilion River. This is near the hillside where the actual orphanage buildings were located— cottages for girls and boys. Mists and lights have been seen at the bridge. So why do they call it Crybaby Bridge? Those who park their cars in the gravel pull-off before the bridge and turn off their cars have gotten small, dusty hand prints on their car windows and windshields. And children's giggles, laughter and crying can be heard when driving away.

Dean's Bridge
9604 Dean Road (Twp Hwy 66)
Wakeman, Ohio 44889
41.348786,-82.344897

Lorain County

Hanging out at Dean's Bridge

Pray you don't see the rope swingin'
because if you do, you're gonna . . .die.

It's an iron-truss span. It might not mean anything to anybody who doesn't have a keen sense of knowledge about historical bridges. For those who do not, in a nutshell, it is old and has some sort of historic value. In fact, it is the last one in the county to survive and is notable enough that both Erie County and Lorain County got together to take care of it so it didn't get demolished.

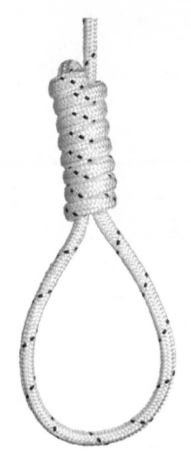

Carriages and cars have both passed over this old bridge. It was built by Massillon Bridge Company all the way back in 1898. Maybe it has even seen a few ghosts cross over, too. Rumor is, a man hung himself on the bridge just after the turn of the century. It took a while to find him, but when they finally pulled him down, they left the rope. It hung there for a long time. If you drive on the bridge some nights, you can see the rope hanging from the girders, swinging back and forth. But there is a slight problem if you do see the rope. You will die not long after.

It is also said that the man did not die so quickly as he hung. As you drive across, you can feel the car move as if the bridge has a heartbeat. Some have also seen a little boy playing by the bridge. When they cross, he vanishes into a fine mist.

By the way. Don't stop your car in the middle of Dean's Bridge and get out of the car. Actually, don't stop at all. It shouldn't have to be said. But as we speak, there is someone out there conjuring up the image of how they will be just a little more courageous than most. They will see themselves opening the door to their car and stepping out on to the gravelly road and running right down the middle to dare the ghost to get them. But don't. It is dangerous. In May of 1974, a 17 year old went to the bridge with a bunch of friends and fell 60 feet down. He was lucky. He lived. But he hurt for a long, long time after. He suffered a bunch of broken bones and was lucky compared to what can happen when most people fall that far.

Spencer Cemetery
99 Jefferson Street
Spencer, Ohio 44275
41.101086,-82.122112

Medina County

By the Lantern Light

According to local lore, an old-fashioned lantern has been seen passing through the cemetery. At times, it is joined by a second light. Some stories relate that the lantern can actually be seen. Hands can pass all around it, but there is no one holding it.

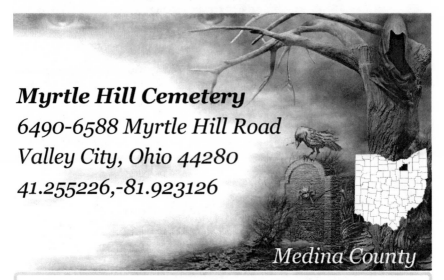

Myrtle Hill Cemetery
6490-6588 Myrtle Hill Road
Valley City, Ohio 44280
41.255226,-81.923126

Medina County

Witch's Grave at Myrtle Hill Cemetery

Some believe the story at Myrtle Hill Cemetery in Valley City. Some don't. According to legend the large granite ball settled on a pedestal with the family name STOSKOPF carved into its base is resting upon a witch's grave. The witch, lore states, murdered her family by poisoning the water in the family well. Then, she threw their lifeless bodies into it as their final grave. Now, with a touch of fingers on the ball, her grave remains cool in the summer and hot in the winter.

In a Medina Gazette article, a local historical society member stated it probably wasn't a grave at all, but simply a marker for the Geroge Stoskopf family buried around the stone. Their first names—George, Helen, Alma and Joseph—are the only imprints on those stones surrounding the ball. Still, no one has dug beneath the stone to prove the story wrong. And folks visit the cemetery, touching the marble gently. Some feel the warmth in winter and coolness in summer. Some don't.

Ohio State Reformatory
100 Reformatory Road
Mansfield, Ohio 44905
40.782686,-82.502875

Richland County

Haunted Ohio State Reformatory

In April 1896, at the same time bills were passed prohibiting the wearing of high hats in theatres which obstruct the view of the stage, it was also passed that the Mansfield Reformatory would be immediately opened. And it was initiated with much fanfare for it had been nearly ten years of construction and funding delays since the brand new cornerstone was first laid. It was said that thousands of people lined the streets, passing out cigars to the 150 inmates who would be moving from the old prison to the new castle-like institute.

Ohio State Reformatory—Mansfield, Ohio.

Mansfield   Reformatory   not   long   after   opening.
Courtesy:Columbus Metro Library

. . . The Reformatory is claimed to be the most modern penal institution in existence. Instead of the narrow, gloomy compartments in which prisoners are ordinarily locked, each cell is roomy, and is provided with a window. The sanitary arrangements are as perfect as it is possible to make them. The

*Reformatory will be occupied by first-term men, convicted of the lighter offenses. The chief object sought is to prevent them from being associated with hardened criminals, which has the effect of counter-acting in the minds of young boys efforts made to reclaim them.—**Our Columbus Letter—The Stark County Democrat., September 10, 1896, Page 6***

The much-awaited reformatory was a large investment for Ohio. The fact that it was self-sustaining like the poor houses and asylums made it a positive asset to the region. Excess funds could help support the institute and it also provided a way for younger men with less offenses to redeem themselves.

Ah, and if ever a place had an impending atmosphere, it would be the monstrous stronghold known as the Ohio State Reformatory. Driving on to the grounds is like entering into the belly of a beast —a fortress-like castle built to withstand escapees and riots and to hold some of Ohio's most corrupt citizens. Built in 1896, the architect for the design was Clevelander Levi T. Scofield. The original idea for this particular prison was for the reform of younger men and restoring them back to society. The Ohio State Reformatory (also called Mansfield Reformatory) took in the mid-level lawbreakers whereas the hardcore criminals were sent to Ohio State Penitentiary in Columbus. Still, funding was an issue from the start. On September 17th, 1896, when the first one-hundred and fifty prisoners were brought to the reformatory, those inmates had to help finish the building. It would be another fourteen years before the prison was complete.

During the time the prison was open, over 154,000 men passed through the gates. As early as 1933, the prison was overcrowded. However, it still remained in use until 1990.

A typical cell inside the prison as it looks today.

So for 94 years, the reformatory swallowed up men who needed redeeming and spit them out reformed.

Well, some were reformed. Many, most likely, were released with good behavior, saw the light of day outside the walls of the prison. Some were not so lucky. They stayed inside the bowels of the huge beast that devoured them. While no one was put to death in this reformatory (the electric chair was at the Ohio Pen), there are 215 men buried in the cemetery-dying from tuberculosis, influenza, violence, and simple diseases cured by antibiotics today.

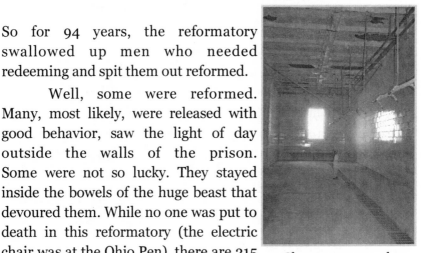

Shower room above. Rows of cells to left.

Within the walls, though, the souls of those who never made it out still linger. There were suicides by hanging and one man is said to set himself on fire.

The Bad Boys of the Mansfield Reformatory

In the summer of 1948, Robert Murl Daniels and 22 year-old John Coulter West, former Ohio State Reformatory prisoners, kidnapped and murdered John Niebel, his wife Nolana and their 21 year-old daughter, Phyllis. John Niebel had been superintendent of the 1600 acre honor farm for 20 years. The revenge-murder had been planned for four years.

Robert Daniels—
Executed 1/3/1949
ODRC Collections

The victims, wearing their nightclothes, had been kidnapped before dawn from their small farm not far from the reformatory. Their nude bodies were found in a cornfield on Fleming Road by a pastor and a youth counselor taking 65 boys on a hike for a Lutheran youth camp eight hours after the abduction. Seeing what appeared to be clothing, the pastor walked closer and saw they were bodies. He returned, telling the boys it was nothing more than slaughtered pigs as not to frighten them.

Phyllis had been beaten and her hair was still held up with the pin curls she had put on before bed. All three had been shot and their clothing was found on the floor of the home. Murderer John Coulter was killed at a roadblock. Robert Daniels died in the electric chair.

Urban Wilford was the first guard murdered in the line of duty at Ohio State Reformatory. It was November 2nd of 1926 and the guard was 72 years old. He was killed by Philip Orleck who was helping a friend escape from the prison. Orleck was later sent to the electric chair.

Philip Orleck—
Executed 07/18/1927
ODRC Collections

Guard Frank Hanger, a 48 year-old guard, was beaten to death with an iron bar by Chester Probaski and Elza Chandler in October of 1932. He was making rounds in the disciplinary block and Chandler was crouching near a cupboard. Chandler was on a 300 day stay in solitary confinement. Both murderers were sent to the electric chair.

Probaski

*Frank B. Hanger of Mt. Vernon, guard at Ohio State Reformatory who is near death in the reformatory hospital after being slugged over the head with an iron bar Sunday night in a futile escape attempt. Elza Chandler prisoner from Urban Crest Franklin county was reported to have confessed that he was the one who wielded the weapon.—**Mansfield News - October 3, 1932 -***

Chandler

The Reformatory Now

The Reformatory operated until 1990 when it was closed. Most of the grounds were demolished. However, the original East (and 6 tiers of the largest free-standing steel cell block in the world) and West Cell Blocks and administration section remain open. This is thanks to the Mansfield Reformatory Preservation Society who took over operation of the building in 1995. They provide tours, ghost walks and ghost hunts to fund the program.

So is the Reformatory Haunted?

Over 200 people were reported to have died at the reformatory including guards killed in escape attempts. Arthur Glattke, a respected superintendent who made much reform in the prison also died of a heart attack in his office. His wife, Helen, was accidently shot in a handgun discharge in the home inside the prison.

It leaves a lot of room for ghosts. And there are ghosts at the reformatory. Audio and digital recordings have turned up clear, distinct voices like: "Please don't touch me", and other audible words. Apparitions are caught in camera pictures taken and people have been poked, prodded and touched.

The Reformatory's Most Haunted Places

East Administration Building —

The Warden and His Family's Quarters

In November of 1950, the warden's wife, Helen Bauer Glattke, died of pneumonia several days after an accidental discharge of a gun in the superintendent's home inside the prison. While reaching into a closet to retrieve a jewelry box, the gun discharged, injuring the woman. Arthur Lewis Glattke, her husband, died following a heart attack suffered in his office on February 10, 1959.

- The voices of people have been heard throughout this area. Footsteps have been heard in the hallways, administrative office where Warden Arthur Lewis Glattke died of a heart attack. His wife, Helen's, voice has been heard in the bedroom and around the closet area where she was accidently shot. There has also been the scent of roses in the rooms. There is also an area where lights from four bedroom windows all come in at once and meet in the exact halfway point of the prison. There is activity there.

3rd Floor West Administration
Chair Room of old priests housing unit and Chapel– Chairs are said to move when the lights are turned out.

West Wing and East Wing Shower and cells- mists and apparitions. Some have felt like they are choking or cannot breath.

East cell block - Pushing, touching, cold spots, images in cameras. Voices.

Solitary Confinement-left - People have been touched, felt cold drafts. A sense of despair and depression may overcome people.

Sub-basement—right—a young boy has been seen.

Our own ghostly shot in administrative area. Appears to be a guard or prisoner walking through the doors behind the real person there. The light shining at the feet is simply sunshine coming through the four windows. We also got a few great EVPs and a voice that said loudly and clearly: "Please don't touch me!".

Akron Civic Theatre
182 South Main Street
Akron, Ohio 44308
41.0805,-81.519631

Summit County

The Protector of Akron Civic Theatre

The theatre was built in 1929 by Marcus Loew, with the look and feel of a Moorish Castle. This older building has been extensively renovated to accommodate performers and visitors and perhaps, along with the living audience, that of one who is dead.

It has been a long-standing legend the theatre is haunted by a previous janitor who died on the premises. He is very protective of the building and watches over it. He appears inside the building, but has also been seen just outside the doors on the sidewalk.

Helltown

Summit County

Hell Town

Okay, so what horrific deeds does a small Ohio community have to accomplish to be nicknamed *Hell Town*? It seems this small, quaint village in Summit County just had to be placed near a large and growing metropolis like Cleveland, along with being settled into one of the most beautiful natural areas in the Midwest. Of course, you have to add in a federal bill to set aside this land for a park along with a property buying spree by the federal government. And lastly, mix in a mass exodus by those many home owners who were booted out. *Now*, you've got a bunch of deep, dark woods with abandoned houses and the rumors start to fly.

It probably isn't the chilling answer you suspected. Well, don't stop here. There is always more to the story. Besides, there really was some pretty scary stuff going on in Hell Town even before it was sucked up by the federal government for park lands.

The focus of many unfounded stories, Cornerstone Family Church on Hines Road is a creditable church.

You see, the actual name of the town was originally Boston, Ohio. It came into existence in 1806 and was a normal community along the Ohio and Erie Canal. It had mills and prospered until around 1974 when much of the land was set aside for a national park. And then all hell broke loose . . .

Krejci Dump was a privately owned dump from 1940 to 1980 near the village of Boston. During this time, the owners began taking in industrial waste, much of it being toxic, along with scrap metal and trash. The land was eventually vacated and during the acquiring of property and land for the Cuyahoga Valley National Park, along with it, the National Park Service purchased this 47 acres of property believing it was simply a junk yard.

After visitors and park personnel began complaining of becoming sick in and near the area, an investigation was completed on the site finding that it did actually contain toxic wastes. *A lot* of toxic wastes. During a massive clean up of the site, signs were posted around the area alerting park visitors of the toxic wastes. Between these signs and the abandoned homes left behind by owners who were forced to relocate when their property was forfeited for the use of the park, folks driving along the roadways began to whisper there was a horrible chemical spill in the region. The homeowners had taken in the toxic wastes and become, well, mutants. The land, then, was only habitable by zombie-like creatures and Satan worshipers.

But crazy urban legends aside, there are a few noteworthy ghost stories in the region . . .

> ### Deep Lock Quarry Park (Railway and Quarry Area)
> 5779 Riverview Road
> Peninsula, Ohio 44264
> 41.230476,-81.554049

Old Valley Railway at Deep Lock Quarry Park

The old Valley Railway runs through Cuyahoga Valley National Park just as it did when it was built in the 1880s. It ambles beside the Cuyahoga River and crosses the water at Deep Lock Quarry Metro Park near the Ohio and Erie Canal Towpath Trail. Where it crosses the river, the headless ghost of a 19th century train conductor has been seen standing by the bridge. Not far away and closer to Peninsula, a ghostly young man has been seen walking along the tracks.

Deep Lock and Canal Area

Just within Deep Lock Quarry Park, Berea Sandstone was once extracted from Deep Rock Quarry to be used to make millstones, canal locks and local structures. It was a dangerous job and more than a few men were killed by falling rock or equipment falling upon them. Now, voices are heard along the trail and nearby at Lock 28 of the Ohio and Erie Canal.

Mater Dolorosa Cemetery

500 West Streetsboro Road
Peninsula Ohio 44264
41.230992,-81.508301

The Mater Dolorosa Cemetery is cozied up beside Cuyahoga Valley National Park's Happy Days Visitors Center. Mostly made up of Irish Catholic settlers, it was established in the late 1860s as a private family plot for the Doud family. Later, it was deeded to the Mother of Sorrows Church. There are approximately 23 people buried here. One of them is Michael Raleigh, an early immigrant who was buried here June 4, 1873. His face shows up on his gravestone.

Michael Raleigh Grave and face to right of cross.

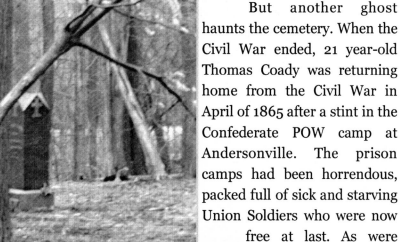

But another ghost haunts the cemetery. When the Civil War ended, 21 year-old Thomas Coady was returning home from the Civil War in April of 1865 after a stint in the Confederate POW camp at Andersonville. The prison camps had been horrendous, packed full of sick and starving Union Soldiers who were now free at last. As were 1,700 other free soldiers, he was crammed into the overloaded Steamship Sultana eager to be rid of the war and get home to his family.

While the ship was pushing along the flooded Mississippi River on April 27, 1865, the boilers exploded near Memphis, Tennessee. Thomas Coady was killed during the explosion, but his body was brought back to his family for burial in Mater Dolorosa Cemetery.

His ghost is said to walk the short paths within the small cemetery. Visitors have seen him peering out behind the graves while they pass by on the trails.

Rogues Hollow

Wayne County

The Legends of Rogues Hollow

Chidester Mill property within Rogues Hollow.

There is a section of land about two miles from Doylestown that is known for its rowdy mining history along with its ghosts. It was first named Chippewa in the early 1800s, at least until Samuel Chidester built his woolen mill in the valley there in 1828. He called it Pleasant Valley. When men first began mining there in the 1840s, folks began calling it Peacock Hollow because the streaks of rainbow colors in the split coal seams. Then, a Doctor Crosby from Akron came in and bought up the mineral rights in some of the land. He was said to name it Rogues Hollow. That's the name that stuck.

Rogues Hollow. As the name implies, it was a rough crowd living there. Since the 1840s, over 50 mines sprang up in the area including the Galehouse Mine, Collier Mine, No. 9 and Woods Mine. Rogues Hollow, tucked deep into the remote area of the northeast, had the right stuff to attract these miners. Old maps show the hollow as having five saloons between Angstang Grist Mill and the Blacksmith Shop including one called the Devil's Saloon. It was a span of less than 3/10 mile.

In all honesty, it was fairly common to see such notes in newspapers throughout Ohio giving credence to Rogues Hollow's reputation as the toughest spot in the country.

> *Frank Herwiek, at whose saloon in Rogues' Hollow, in Wayne county, the riot occurred last week, was arrested Friday, charged with shooting with intent to kill. He waived examination and gave bail for his appearance at court.*
> **The Stark Democrat. Canton, Ohio. May 5, 1883.**

> *Peter Anfang, citizen of the aristocratic region known as Rogues Hollow near Doylestown, was beaten to death by George Dieble, Wednesday of last week. Alleged that Anfang accused Dieble's brother of seducing his daughter.*
> **The Stark County Democrat. January 12, 1882. Our Sister Cities.**

The Akron daily Democrat on March 31, 1900, would describe it as this:

> *Midway between Clinton and Doylestown is a valley which was nicknamed Rogues Hollow, over 30 years ago, when the first coal mines were opened. The opening of the mines naturally drew the toughest element from foreign countries. Saloons and lawlessness reigned supreme. After the men received their pay on Saturday night they would spend their time in fighting. Five or six bare fist fights were no unusual thing. Authorities were wholly unable to enforce the law, and a stranger's life was always in danger at night in that vicinity. After the mines were abandoned, the place was deserted and now it is a peaceful locality.*
> **The Akron daily Democrat on March 31, 1900. Rogues Hollow Was a Dangerous Place.**

Peaceful now or not, Rogues Hollow's notorious past left behind a wide array of ghosts, each embodying the very existence they played a part of in life. . . .

The Ghosts of the Miners

The roads around Rogue's Hollow like Fraze and Clinton Roads were once travelled by many miners.

With more than five mines in the area, it shouldn't be a shock to know that once in a while, the ghostly sound of pick against coal wall is heard ringing in the air. The sound of mules pulling carts and the now eerie blast of dynamite from long ago are heard once in a while. Even the shadowy figures of miners have been seen where the old mines once stood.

The Ghost of the Headless Horse at the Ghost Oak Tree
40.945563,-81.666067

Russell W. Frey who wrote the *Rogues Hollow History and Legends* (this can still be purchased from the Chippewa-Rogues Hollow Historical Society - chippewarogueshollow.org) tells of a story passed down by the Walsh family who originally owned Walsh's tavern in the Rogue's Hollow. You see, there was an old Oak Tree on Clinton Road that ran from Clinton through Rogue's Hollow and then to Doylestown. It was huge and had branches hanging down over the road. Those who knew about the low-hanging branches knew to duck down in their wagons or on horseback when they crested the hill just before Fraze Road. This was especially so in winter when the ice froze on the branches and pulled them lower.

The Ghost Oak and the Headless Horse were once found at the top of the Clinton Road Hill near Fraze.

There was a legend about the old tree due to these low branches. It was called the Ghost Oak Tree because one night a tall horse was galloping along the road, collided with the tree and was killed. His ghost was seen under the tree for years, a dusky shadow beneath the limbs.

The ghostly horse was seen by Micky Walsh (he would have been about 20 years-old in 1889) who worked for Wood's Mine, tending the mules that carried coal from the mines. One day he was returning from Clinton after taking the mules to the blacksmith to be shod. Caught up in socializing in town, he did not leave until the road was dark. It was dangerous enough because of the roughnecks around riding the roads of Rogue's Hollow after dusk. But just as he was upon the tree driving the mules, he saw what he swore was the devil, himself, with two red glowing eyes sitting on the low branch.

Days later, when he returned to show his friends, they swore they saw the devil sitting on the Ghost Horse beneath the old oak tree. Although the tree is now gone, the horse is said to still be around. He has been seen along the darker parts of Clinton Road and into Rogues Hollow.

Twin Ghosts
40.965641,-81.694 to
40.954266,-81.684473

The Twin Ghosts were seen along Clinton Road, just outside Doylestown by George Ringler. It was about 1/10th mile outside town. Although it was boasted by two men who lived along the street they had dressed up to scare folks, others had seen the two white ghosts throughout the years, pop up and follow them a bit, then disappear.

Crybaby Bridge
40.941071,-81.67521

If you take Clinton Road from Doylestown and hop on Clinton Road going south, you'll eventually find Galehouse Road and a small bridge. It is here you will discover not only Rogue's Hollow Historical Park, but also a few ghostly legends passed down over the years. The little bridge you see spanning Silver Creek is Wayne County's notorious Crybaby Bridge. The story goes that a young woman was spurned by her sweetheart when he found out she was pregnant. When the child was born, she tossed it into the cold waters. If you stand on the bridge, you can hear the child's wails. And you might even see the mournful mama. She stands along the edge, staring into the water, forever lamenting her awful feat.

> **Chidester Mill**
> **117514 Galehouse Road**
> **Doylestown, Ohio 44230**
> **40.941365,-81.67536**
> **chippewarogueshollow.org**

Then: Chidester Mill and Dye House in its early days. Now a unique museum and hiking trails make this a great day trip.

And then, there is the Ghost of Chidester's Mill just across the bridge. The woolen mill, along with a sawmill and a dye house, was started by Samuel and Ephriam Chidester. It was in business from 1828 to 1888 and passed down through the family. During the early times it was in use, a young man was accidently killed while making repairs on the mill. He fell into the wheel and was crushed to death. Many who lived in Rogues Hollow said they saw the man return in the evenings long after he was dead as if to finish his work he never got to complete. In 1922, the original building was torn down and replaced by the building used as a museum today. Chippewa Township now leases the property and has opened it to the public as the Chippewa Nature Preserve and the Rogues Hollow  Historical Park. Still, the young man's ghost is said to roam the property, returning at dusk to work on the mill.

River Styx Trestle
256-262 E Ohio Avenue
Rittman, Ohio 44270
40.974941,-81.772252

Wayne County

Ghost Train Over River Styx

The Erie west-bound passenger train No. 5 was due in Mansfield at 8:56 a.m. on March 22, 1899. It was about a half mile past Rittman and was heading toward Sterling at a rate of 60 miles per hour. It did not make it on time. Some time between 7:30 a.m. and 8:00 a.m., just as it crossed the trestle over a small stream named the River Styx (Styx River), the train jumped the track and rolled over. All the cars, save a dining car, were derailed. Alexander Logan, the 48 year-old engineer was crushed beneath the train.

Seven months later, a local Rittman doctor was returning home with a friend after visiting a patient. Just outside town, the two leisurely watched a train working its way down the tracks.

It was almost to the short trestle running over the River Styx, when the shrill whistle caused them to turn. Then, to their alarm, just as it got to the trestle, they heard the engine engage as if it were being placed in reverse and burst into great flames and smoke. The crash of metal and wood resounded in the air. Shrieks came from the wreckage

---

HAUNTED. *River Styx Bridge. Fearful Sights Witnessed at the Place Where Engineer Logan Lost His Life. Phantom Train Dashes Down Steep Grade.*

Frightful Wreck Reenacted Every Night -Strange Story.

The ill-fated train, on which Engineer Alex. W. Logan lost his life, is said to haunt the bridge over the River Styx near Rittman. It was at this place that he went to his heroic death last spring. The frightful wreck caused great excitement in this city. There were a large number of Akron people on No. 5 that morning. Local citizens recall the circumstances surrounding the brave sacrifice made by Engineer Logan, whose steady nerve saved the passengers behind him. That which follows is taken from the Wadsworth Banner of Friday :

Several Rittman people are very much excited at what has occurred at the Styx bridge over the Erie at that place during the past week, and what they term was the appearance of a phantom train. The first appearance of this awe-inspiring marvelous apparition, was on Saturday night, and was witnessed by Dr. Faber and a companion. The doctor had been out east to visit a patient and was leisurely driving along about 11 o'clock when his attention was attracted by the noise of a swiftly moving train. He casually watched the train and saw its glaring headlight and dense clouds of smoke rolling up from the smokestack.

No particular attention was taken of the train, but just before it reached the bridge the shrill whistle of the engine caused the men to glance back. On came the train with the speed of the wind as it swept down the grade, throwing out great streaks. Just then was heard the "chuck, chuck" of the engine, as if she had been reversed. On further investigation a frightful sight met their gaze. The train was enveloped in great clouds of dust and smoke and huge flames of fire shot up in every direction, and immense volumes of steam making a terrific noise shot up from the engine, and the noise of creaking timbers and breaking iron bars was plainly heard, but above all came the shrieks of those pinioned beneath the wreckage. The noise was plainly heard by a number of others. Spellbound at the sight before them Faber and his companion started immediately for the railroad, thinking that a frightful wreck had occurred. Imagine their surprise when they reached the bridge and found everything perfectly quiet, no sign of a wrecked train, and not even a ripple upon the placid surface of the Styx.

The men hurried to town and related their experience, but could not induce anyone else to visit the spot, so strong is the belief down there that this place is haunted or some evil spirit lingers about the bridge. Near there the ill-fated train 5 jumped the track last spring and the engineer was killed, ever since which time many people have been afraid to pass over this stretch of track after night.

Akron Daily Democrat. October 28, 1899. Haunted. River Styx Bridge.

Over the next year, more people reported seeing or hearing the ghost train following its fateful path across the River Styx train trestle. By April of 1901, a panic was nearly induced when more citizens of the town reported seeing a train wreck occur when no genuine train was nearby.

UNCANNY VISITANT

The Forerunner of Some Dire Disaster.

Rittman People Are Bordering Nervous Prostration Because of Another Appearance of the Phantom Train.

. . . *A week go the phantom train was seen by three reputable citizens of Rittman, J. B. Ewing, Amos Goldner, and a man named Fielding were walking along the Erie tracks near the trestle when they were startled by a shrill whistle behind them. Turning, they beheld the headlight of a train bearing down upon them from the East. By the moon's light they could plainly see the great column of black smoke belching from the stack.*

The three decided it was Erie passenger No. 1 trying to make up time, by the way she was coming. They all stepped a safe distance from the rails and waited for the train to pass. As it struck a slight curve in the track the men could plainly see that the locomotive pulled a baggage car, mail car, and three passenger coaches. Through the coach windows light from the interior was stealing. Shortly before the train reached the trestle it whistled again shrilly for brakes, and sparks began to fly from the wheels, as they ground upon the steel rail, locked by the brake application.

The men were wondering at the sudden stopping of the train, when it shot out on the trestle and plunged into the river. They plainly heard the cracking of the trestle timbers, the hissing of escaping steam, and the shrieks and groans of the pinioned passengers. The astonished onlookers stood for a moment petrified, and then ran down over the embankment to the edge of the stream into which the train had plunged.

When they arrived upon the bank they were amazed to find that not a ripple disturbed the placid surface of the water. Looking up, they were surprised to find that the timbers of the trestle were stable and intact. The place was as quiet as death, and although the three men are possessed of an average amount of courage, they crept away from the haunted place with the cries of the dying in their ears, and hurried toward the town.

These men might have doubted their own senses if it had not been for the fact that they wore hailed by residents of houses nearby who had heard the noise of the wrecked train and asked if there had not been another wreck at the Styx bridge. . . The uncanny visitant has caused intense excitement among the residents of Rittman. . .

Akron Daily Democrat., April 23, 1901, Page 5. Uncanny Visitant.

Some thought the ghost train to be a forerunner to some great disaster which would occur in Rittman. Considering the name of the stream that the No. 5 train wrecked over had the haunting name of River Styx, it probably seemed plausible. But the name only matched its early years before the towns were built around it. When the land in the southeastern part of Medina County was first surveyed, it was called a place of wilderness and dark trails, wild animals and snakes. The land and small community was deemed a mirror image of Greek Mythology's River Styx that encircles the dark world of Hades. The name stuck.

But if the train was an omen for some ill fortune amidst the land once compared to the terrifying underworld, it never came to pass. Rittman is still alive and well and a thriving community. The river still runs beneath the trestle and trains run above. And perhaps, on moonless nights, the sound of the No. 5 still makes its fateful run along the tracks and the screams still resound in the air.

The River Styx
256-262 E Ohio Avenue
Rittman, Ohio 44270
40.974941,-81.772252

Wayne County

A Chippewa Legend of the River Styx

Before the spirit of the No. 5 train haunted the area around the bridge in Rittman, another legend was already woven into otherworldly fabric of the region. It was in the early years when settlers were just beginning to discover the beauty of the region, and native Indians still wandered the thick backwoods and wild areas. It was during the time that the Chippewa used the River Styx to traverse this section of Ohio. It was so widely known, the Akron Daily Democrat retold the story in the spring of 1901. It seems one day in the year of 1821, while a group of these Indians were along the river, they were surprised by a party of Delaware, Choctaws and Mingos. A battle ensued and a young warrior was killed who had been about to marry the daughter of an elderly chief. The young Chippewa women was driven mad by the loss of her betrothed. She left her family and disappeared into the woods around the River Styx.

The Chippewa had a legend that the spirit of the young woman would return to the creek at midnight on the 21st of each October. In 1827, two men tested the theory and found out the truth ...

. . . *It was on the night of October 21, 1827, two young men decided to test the truth of this indian tradition, so they set out from the mouth of the Styx north of where the railroad bridge now stands when they concluded they were far enough and they stood still to await the events. Dark clouds obscured the skies, owls hooted, and wolves snarled and barked away in the jungles. Each stood motionless for some time busy with his thoughts. Precisely at 12 o'clock there shot out from the opposite side the stream, or pond, it was then, a bark canoe, bearing a headlight, such as was used by hunters in those days, in its bow, while in the stern sat a beautiful indian maiden of about 20 summers, dressed after the fashion of her tribe. The canoe glided around over the pond like a bird until the third time when it entered the channel and shot down stream. The two young men breathlessly watched the canoe as its headlight began to disappear down the creek when the spell was broken by the low plaintive indian death song coming up the channel from the direction taken by the phantom. Suddenly the canoe shifted around and glided back toward the center of the pond, and to the consternation of the young men the canoe turned bottom upward and all disappeared together, and the young men were left alone in the blackness of the night, trembling in every nerve and lost little time in getting to their homes.*

Akron Daily Democrat., May 02, 1901, Page 5

Calvary Cemetery:
http://www.touristlink.com/united-states/calvary-cemetery/overview.html
Fisher, Jeffrey. Ghosts of Cleveland: The Haunted Locations of Cleveland,
Ohio Amazon Digital Services, Inc.

Joseph Thompkins and Mary Pauli:
-February 2, 1913. Cleveland Plain Dealer— Who'll Make This Ghost Happy—
Historical Archives.
-City of Cleveland Oh Dept of Parks & Public Property. Register of
Interrments.www.rootsweb.ancestry.com/~ohcdrt/clecems/images/
wo_01_015.jpg
-http://wcfcle.org/interment/wcfiis_detail.php?l=Tomkins&f=Joseph&b=1855
-02-15%
2000:00:00&r=000603&s=0&x=Tomkins&y=joseph&d=000603&a=C&t=N
-cemetery map: Section 83—http://www.wcfcle.org/maps/Woodland_Maps/
WC83.pdf
-cemetery map: Section 8

Mad Butcher of Kingsbury:
-Beck, Heather. Heather's Halloween:Mad Butcher of Kingsbury Run – The
Cleveland Torso Murders. Retrieved 2014, from http://
www.heathershalloween.com/mad-butcher-of-kingsbury-run-the-cleveland-
torso-murders/
- http://images.ulib.csuohio.edu/cdm/singleitem/collection/press/id/56/
rec/37
- www.clevelandpolicemuseum.org/collections/kingsburyrun.html
-America's Strangest Murder Mystery. Hammond Times. 1937-07-18
-Torso Slayer Defies Expert Classification. Coshocton Tribune (Coshocton,
Ohio) October 6th 1938
- The Kingsbury Run Murders or Cleveland Torso Murders BY Marilyn Bardsley
- Coshocton Tribune (Coshocton, Ohio) October 6th 1938
- http://www.crimelibrary.com/serial_killers/unsolved/kingsbury/
index_1.html
-Google Places: Cleveland Torsos Murder Map- http://goo.gl/maps/tTtwh
-www.findagrave.com/cgi-bin/fg.cgi?page=gr&GRid=18878976

Squire's Castle:
-Reed, Margaret. North Chagrin Has Castle and Trails. Cleveland Plain Dealer.
August 16, 1939.

Drury Castle:
-Petkovic, John. "Ghosts, Haunts, and Urban Legends." Cleveland Plain Dealer.
October 31, 2000.
-Trickey, Erick. Cleveland Magazine. http://www.clevelandmagazine.com -
Francis E. Drury House /1910/. December, 2011
- Willoughby Area Paranormal Education and Research Society, Cathi Weber,
Trina O'Dell
-Scary For Kids, Cleveland Ohio. www.scaryforkids.com/cleveland-ohio/

Big Four Railroad:
-http://www.interment.net/data/us/oh/cuyahoga/calvary/calvary_f.htm
-http://images.ulib.csuohio.edu/cdm/ref/collection/postcards/id/571
-THE PENNSYLVANIA RAILROAD'S CLEVELAND DOCK. Cleveland State University
Library.http://web.ulib.csuohio.edu/speccoll/prrcd/Prrchap2.html
-ancestry.com

Freight House:
Michael Rotman, "Superior Viaduct," *Cleveland Historical*, accessed July 19, 2014,
http://clevelandhistorical.org/items/show/65.
http://www.interment.net/data/us/oh/cuyahoga/calvary/calvary_f.htm

Cuyahoga:
http://cleveland.about.com/od/clevelandhistory/ss/hauntedclev_2.htm
National Register Information System". National Register of Historic Places. National
Park Service. 2009-03-13. Armory image: Courtesy Columbus Metropolitan Library

Lake View Cemetery:
http://www.deadohio.com/lakeview1.**htm**
http://www.findagrave.com/cgi-bin/fg.cgi?page=cr&CRid=41762
Agora:
Encyclopedia of Cleveland History: Agora Ballroom
http://www.clevelandagora.com/History
Erie Street Cemetery:
Case Western Reserve University
Erie Street Cemetery By John D. Cimperman
Franklin Castle:
The Times Recorder: Jan 19, 1975 - Zanesville, Ohio
Tiedemann House (Franklin Castle) by: Jim Dubelko—
http://clevelandhistorical.org/items/show/531#.UgBTVLbD_cs
www.hauntedamericatours.com: http://www.hauntedamericatours.com/
hauntedhouses/franklincastle/
Findagrave.com—http://www.findagrave.com/cgi-bin/fg.cgi?
page=gsr&GSiman=1&GScid=645569&GSfn=&GSln=Tiedemann
Ancestry.com—Tiedemann, Hannes
Cuyahoga Valley National Park:
-Summit Metro Parks. www.summitmetroparks.org/parksandtrails/
deeplockquarry.aspx
-The Belmont Chronicle. St. Clairsville, Ohio. October 16, 1890.Happenings of
the week—Two Killed in Derrick Fall at Quarry.
-archiver.rootsweb.ancestry.com/th/read/OHSUMMIT/2001-04/0986914700
-Arizona"s New Immigration Law; The Tale of Two Soldiers-
uselesstriviaandmindlessrants.blogspot.com/2010/04/arizonas-new-
immigration-law-tale-of.html
-deadohio.com
-Brecksville—Summit County Map: 1874
Akron Civic Theatre:
-Mark, S., & McGuire, M. M. (Eds.). Weird U.S. (). Barnes & Noble Publishing.
Spencerville:
-Gilbert, K. Haunted? United Methodist Church. Even Wesleys heard 'bumps in
night'. http://www.umc.org/news-and-media/haunted-even-wesleys-heard-
bumps-in-night.
River Styx Bridge Train Wreck:
-ENGINEER KILLED And Fireman Fatally Injured by a Wreck on the Erie.
Mansfield News, Mansfield, OH 22 Mar 1899
-Rittman, OH Train Wreck, Mar 1899. NEEDS LAUNDERING. Badly Damaged
Mail Brought in From the Wreck at Rittman. Mansfield News, Mansfield, OH 23
Mar 1899
-Milton Township Atlas: Wayne County 1897
Rogues Hollow:
-CHIPPEWA ROGUES HOLLOW NATURE PRESERVE
and HISTORICAL PARK. 17500 Galehouse Road, Doylestown OH.
www.chippewarogueshollow.org/
-Locher, Paul. Coal mining brings prosperity to Doylestown area. Daily Record.
-Frey, Russell. "Rogues' Hollow, History and Legends".
-Chippewa Township, Doylestown, Centerburg, Fox Lake Jct., Marshallville,
Easton, Hametown Atlas: Wayne County 192x W. W. Hixson and co.
River Styx Bridge Train Wreck:
-ENGINEER KILLED And Fireman Fatally Injured by a Wreck on the Erie.
Mansfield News, Mansfield, OH 22 Mar 1899
-Rittman, OH Train Wreck, Mar 1899. NEEDS LAUNDERING. Badly Damaged
Mail Brought in From the Wreck at Rittman. Mansfield News, 23 Mar 1899.
-Milton Township Atlas: Wayne County 1897

Character Images:

21 Crows. Deyan Georgiev, © Elnur, © captblack76, © Antonio Gravante , © jorgophotography© Anelina - Fotolia.com, gromovataya,© Andrey Kiselev, © giorgiomtb - Fotolia.com, © Wampa , © afxhome , © olesha - © Artem Merzlenko, © aleshin, © captblack76 © maksimshirkov © Jag_cz , © darkbird , © jorgophotography, © Nando Machado © romantsubin - Fotolia.com © mozgova - Fotolia.com, © Can Stock Photo Inc. / refocusphoto, Attribution - Print© Can Stock Photo Inc. / Anke © Can Stock Photo Inc. / Anke © Can Stock Photo Inc. / oneword , © Alex Tihonov - Fotolia.com, © Mikhail Pogosov - Fotolia.com, © Can Stock Photo Inc. / wtamas © daynamore - Fotolia.com,© Can Stock Photo Inc. / stokkete © Can Stock Photo Inc. / chainatp, © Can Stock Photo Inc. / Icenando Credit / Attribution - Print
© Can Stock Photo Inc. / Anke, Print© Can Stock Photo Inc. / ocusfocus, © Can Stock Photo Inc. / HPW,Can Stock Photo Inc. / bluemonster © ysbrandcosijn - Fotolia.com © ysbrandcosijn - Fotolia.com, © Aija Krodere - Fotolia.com © jorgophotography - Fotolia.com, © sad - Fotolia.com © Christopher Meder - Fotolia.com © Alex Tihonov - Fotolia.com © Demian - Fotolia.com © snapaway78 - Fotolia.com © eldadcarin - Fotolia.com © Shchipkova Elena - Fotolia.com © mrcats - Fotolia.com © ysbrandcosijn - Fotolia.com © Rob Byron - Fotolia.com© ysbrandcosijn - Fotolia.com
© Scott Griessel - Fotolia.com, © Netfalls - Fotolia.com ©[Dmitriy Cherevko]/123RF.COM , ©[Sheri Armstrong]/123RF.COM, ©[fotomaximum']/123RF.COM, ©[Belchonock]/123RF.COM,© [Burand]/123RF.COM, ©[Elena Yutilova]/123RF.COM , ©[evdoha]/123RF.COM, © anyka]/123RF.COM ©[Andrey Kiselev]/123RF.COM ©[araraadt]/123RF.COM © [massonforstock]/123RF.COM , [jorgophotography]/123RF.COM

CPSIA information can be obtained
at www.ICGtesting.com
Printed in the USA
LVOW12s1614021017
550899LV00005B/859/P

9 781940 087108